Quit While You're Alive . . .

He ran into the immovable wall of Longarm's right hand. This time he went down, sprawling onto his back. He had yet to land a solid blow on Longarm, while he himself was bloody and covered with dirt and bits of weeds.

"You son of a bitch." It came out as much a moan as an accusation.

The fellow struggled to his knees and glared balefully up at Longarm.

"That's enough, kid," Longarm said calmly. "I don't wanna hurt you." He turned away and reached out to Bea for his things. He had his Stetson on and was about to take his gunbelt from her when Bea's right hand flashed and a four barreled derringer, the gambler's special, appeared in her hand with a magician's speed.

The little pistol barked, and a tiny hole appeared in the big fellow's forehead.

He blinked. Then went to his knees and toppled face forward into the dirt, a revolver that had been in his hand falling uselessly with him.

"He was going to shoot you in the back, Custis," she explained and handed Longarm his gunbelt and coat. "He had the pistol in his pocket."

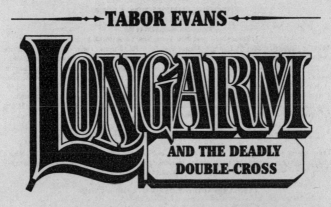

TABOR EVANS

LONGARM

AND THE DEADLY DOUBLE-CROSS

JOVE BOOKS, NEW YORK

THE BERKLEY PUBLISHING GROUP
Published by the Penguin Group
Penguin Group (USA) Inc.
375 Hudson Street, New York, New York 10014, USA

Penguin Group (Canada), 90 Eglinton Avenue East, Suite 700, Toronto, Ontario M4P 2Y3, Canada (a division of Pearson Penguin Canada Inc.) • Penguin Books Ltd., 80 Strand, London WC2R 0RL, England • Penguin Group Ireland, 25 St. Stephen's Green, Dublin 2, Ireland (a division of Penguin Books Ltd.) • Penguin Group (Australia), 250 Camberwell Road, Camberwell, Victoria 3124, Australia (a division of Pearson Australia Group Pty. Ltd.) • Penguin Books India Pvt. Ltd., 11 Community Centre, Panchsheel Park, New Delhi—110 017, India • Penguin Group (NZ), 67 Apollo Drive, Rosedale, Auckland 0632, New Zealand (a division of Pearson New Zealand Ltd.) • Penguin Books (South Africa) (Pty.) Ltd., 24 Sturdee Avenue, Rosebank, Johannesburg 2196, South Africa

Penguin Books Ltd., Registered Offices: 80 Strand, London WC2R 0RL, England

This is a work of fiction. Names, characters, places, and incidents either are the product of the author's imagination or are used fictitiously, and any resemblance to actual persons, living or dead, business establishments, events, or locales is entirely coincidental.

LONGARM AND THE DEADLY DOUBLE-CROSS

A Jove Book / published by arrangement with the author

PRINTING HISTORY
Jove edition / August 2012

Copyright © 2012 by Penguin Group (USA) Inc.
Cover illustration by Milo Sinovcic.

ISBN: 978-0-515-15103-9

JOVE®
Jove Books are published by The Berkley Publishing Group,
a division of Penguin Group (USA) Inc.,
375 Hudson Street, New York, New York 10014.
JOVE® is a registered trademark of Penguin Group (USA) Inc.
The "J" design is a trademark of Penguin Group (USA) Inc.

PRINTED IN THE UNITED STATES OF AMERICA

10 9 8 7 6 5 4 3 2 1

ALWAYS LEARNING   **PEARSON**

Chapter 1

"Oh! Yes, yes. More, sweetheart. Harder, please. Faster. Yes!" Longarm wriggled and squirmed in a paroxysm of sheer ecstasy. "More. Please, more."

"Mr. Long. Really. Haven't I scratched that itch enough?" the girl said as she vigorously rubbed Longarm between the shoulder blades.

"Sorry, dear. I don't mean to tire you out. But maybe we could, um, scratch each other a little more tonight after you get off work."

The girl blushed and dropped her eyes demurely. Longarm laughed and said, "Here? Eight o'clock or thereabouts?"

He was teasing. Only that. But damned if she didn't nod. Blush even more furiously. Then turn and hurry away without again looking directly at him.

"Well, I'll be a son of a bitch," he mumbled softly to himself as he dug into his pocket for a coin to cover the cost of breakfast plus a generous tip for the pretty waitress. He deposited the cartwheel on the table beside his plate and empty coffee cup, grabbed his brown Stetson from the seat of the chair opposite his, and headed for the door.

The tall deputy United States marshal stepped out onto the sidewalk along the south side of Colfax Avenue in downtown Denver, paused there, and settled the hat comfortably onto his head.

A pair of young women who were setting out on the important business of shopping for new hats of their own turned their heads and gave Longarm frankly approving glances. That was really no wonder. Custis Long was a striking figure.

His look was ruggedly masculine, definitely not the pretty boy sort that some found to be attractive. He was well over six feet in height with brown hair, brown eyes, and a broad sweep of dark brown handlebar mustache. Years spent in the saddle had given him a deep tan and a horseman's narrow hips and powerful thighs.

He wore a brown tweed coat, brown corduroy trousers, and a light brown calfskin vest, with a sturdy watch chain across his flat belly. On one end of that chain was the expected pocket watch, but on the other was hidden a .41-caliber derringer.

Longarm wore calf-high, black, stovepipe cavalry boots with low walking heels, and around his waist was a black gunbelt and holster, the holster carried just to the left of his belt buckle and canted for a cross-draw. It held a .45-caliber double-action Colt revolver. And in the unlikely event that the guns failed, he had a folding knife in his trousers pocket.

He took a moment to enjoy the view of the young women—lovely but probably regrettably chaste—as they passed down the street, then he turned to his right and proceeded down Colfax toward the U.S. Mint and, across the side street from it, the Federal Building where United States Marshal William Vail had his offices.

It was a building Longarm was long familiar with, as he had been Billy Vail's top deputy for some years now.

He stifled a yawn and took the stone steps up to the double doors of the Federal Building two at a time, then let himself in and crossed the lobby to the door to the marshal's office.

"Mornin', Henry," he said to Billy Vail's clerk as he

entered, removing his hat and tossing it onto the hat rack in the corner. He did not bother looking toward Henry's desk to see if the man was at work already. There was no need. Henry was always there ahead of Longarm's arrival. Always.

"Good morning yourself, Longarm. Are you ill?"

Longarm turned and looked at the mousy, bespectacled fellow—Henry's appearance was deceiving; Longarm knew him to be as tough as any of the deputies. "Huh? Me? Why?"

Henry smiled. "Because you are on time. I can't remember the last time that happened."

"Last March," Longarm said quickly.

"Yes, but that doesn't count. That time you stayed up playing cards all night and came to work drunk."

"The hell I did," Longarm retorted. "I stayed up all night with that chesty redhead that deals faro at the Chinaman's. It was her I was playing, not her cards."

"My apologies," Henry said with a chuckle. "Anyway, it's good that you are here. The boss wants to see you."

"He's gonna give me something t'do? Good. I been laying around in the city more'n long enough."

Longarm stopped to lightly knock on the door into Billy Vail's private office, waited to hear the resulting "come," and then stepped inside, closing the door behind him. Not that there was really any need for privacy. Whatever the assignment, Henry would already know every detail. And probably had any travel or expense vouchers made out ahead of time.

"Yes, sir," Longarm said smartly, stopping just short of snapping his heels together and giving the boss a salute.

Chapter 2

William Vail, marshal of the Denver District, United States Department of Justice, was seated behind his broad, uncluttered desk, the morning sun shining off the top and one side of his bald head. With his pink, freshly shaved cheeks, the man looked positively cherubic, but Billy Vail's looks were every bit as deceiving as his clerk's. Billy Vail was a former Texas Ranger and in his own right was one salty son of a bitch. He knew his way around six-guns and bad men.

Now Billy carefully looked at Longarm, pulled a watch from his vest pocket and consulted it, gave the watch a shake and held it to his ear, then grunted softly and put the watch away.

"You never fail to surprise me, Custis," he said.

"Aw, c'mon, Boss. It ain't that rare for me to get here early," Longarm protested.

Billy grunted again. "In point of fact, Custis, you are not early. You are, however, on time. That is the amazement." He gestured toward one of the two wooden armchairs set in front of his desk, and Longarm sat. "I have a job for you."

"Nothin' boring, I hope," Longarm said.

"Hardly that," Vail told him. "I received a telegram

delivered to my home this morning. An urgent request from the post office that we investigate a theft that occurred this morning shortly after midnight. Between twelve-twenty and three-fifteen as closely as they can determine."

"A break-in?" Longarm asked.

Vail shook his head. "A train robbery. Union Pacific Number 34 was held up while it was still under way."

"That's damn strange, Boss," Longarm put in. "Those postal messengers lock up tight and don't open for anybody, not for hell or high water."

"They would like to ask the messenger about exactly that," Billy said, "except the man is dead. For some reason he did open the door and let one or more robbers into the mail car. They took at least one bag of mail, perhaps more. The post office is checking their agents at the previous stops to find out just what went on and what came off.

"They find it especially interesting that not all the mail was taken. Only a selected bag or bags."

"So the thieves had to know what they expected to find in those bags and had to know which bags was which."

"That is another thing," Billy said. "The post office wants to know where those particular bags originated."

"When they do, I'll be interested to find out myself," Longarm said. "Could give me an idea of what's up. Somebody had to know something. Somebody had to tell somebody else. If I find one somebody, it might could lead me to the other somebodies. How'd they stop the train when they had their mailbags then?"

"That is another interesting thing," Billy said. "They didn't."

Longarm's eyebrows went up.

"The train operated its normal schedule. Mail had been delivered to Cheyenne at twelve-twenty and the train stopped again at Medicine Bow at three-fifteen. The conductor expected to take on mail and make a delivery there.

That is when they discovered the robbery. And the dead express clerk."

Longarm frowned in thought. "Whoever got those bags and killed the clerk could've tossed the bags off and jumped behind them without bein' seen."

"Yes. Or they could have thrown the bag, or bags, off to an accomplice on the ground, then returned to a passenger coach and continued on to Medicine Bow. You should check on all the passengers who left the train there, I think."

"This ain't gonna be easy, Boss," Longarm said.

Billy smiled. "If I expected it to be easy, Custis, I would do it myself."

"All right then. Any special instructions?" Longarm stood.

"No, none. Henry will give you your expense vouchers. But do get on this right away. That telegram coming in the middle of the night suggests that the postal service is particularly worried about this matter. But then they should be. One of their own has been murdered, and they not only fail to know by whom, they cannot understand how the thieves got into the mail car."

"Give me a little time an' I'll tell 'em," Longarm said confidently, turning to leave the boss's office.

He would have to remember to tell the little blond waitress in Starr's Café that he would not be coming by for her this evening, Longarm told himself.

Then he would have to stop by at his boardinghouse to grab the carpetbag he always kept packed and ready. After that he'd need to work out what would be the quickest way to reach Medicine Bow.

That would be by train, he supposed, and the schedules being what he remembered them to be, his best bet there would be to take the morning express east to Julesburg, connect with the Union Pacific there, and roll west through Cheyenne to Medicine Bow.

Right, he decided. That would be the quickest. It would be slow, but even so it would be his quickest way.

Longarm had that worked out by the time he stopped in front of Henry's desk to collect the vouchers Henry already had made out for him.

Chapter 3

"Shit!" Longarm woke from the half sleep he had been in, slumped in a corner of one of the railroad coach's very hard wooden seats.

He came awake and sat upright, annoyed with himself. He had forgotten, dammit, to go by the café and tell that pretty little waitress that he would not be able to pick her up for their date. Damn it all, anyway. Now she would be mad at him, and there was every likelihood that he had blown his chances to get inside her bloomers. And she was such a pretty little thing too.

Across the aisle a young mother with two kids clinging to her skirts gave him a dirty look. She must have heard his exclamation, he thought. "Shit," he said again. Louder this time. The woman turned red and looked away, covering the ears of the older kid, who was probably six or thereabouts.

Longarm scowled and reached inside his coat for a cheroot. He snapped a lucifer alight and applied it to the tip of the cheroot, then slouched into the end of the seat again. It would be at least an hour before they reached Julesburg.

He waited until the train was completely stopped, not willing to join the herd who seemed to think if they got up and stood in the aisle that would somehow help them get off quicker; then he stood up and pulled his carpetbag down off the overhead shelf. The aisle empty, he walked forward past the iron plate where a coal-burning stove would be placed in winter and leisurely stepped down.

It was a short hansom ride to the Union Pacific depot, where he inquired about the 2:10 to Cheyenne and points west.

"She's on time, mister. Want to buy a ticket on her?"

Longarm smiled and shook his head. There were not a great many perks that came with the badge but being able to ride free on any conveyance that carried the United States mail was one. All he would have to do to secure his ride would be to show his badge to the conductor; no ticket was necessary.

The snippy woman with the two brats was traveling westward also, he found, when he stepped out onto the platform to wait for the next train west. He tried to ignore her, but the older kid seemed to be fascinated by the sight of him. The boy kept alternately staring at Longarm and whispering in his mother's ear.

After ten minutes or so the woman gave the boy a swat on his backside and set him firmly onto a bench. Then she marched over to where Longarm was sitting, planted her hands firmly on her hips, and said, "You are bothering my son, sir."

Longarm gave her a sour look—she was not all that attractive although he supposed she might look good enough if the lights were all out—and said, "Lady, I ain't said shit since we all of us got here, so what's the kid bothered about?"

Her face clouded over and her nose hiked another couple inches into the air. She probably suspected, correctly as it turned out, that his choice of language was deliberate. "It is your gun, sir."

"My revolver? Lady, I haven't pointed it at him or nothing, so what's the problem?"

She sniffed. Loudly. "It is the sight of the nasty thing, sir. Small children should not be subjected to such evil, so I am asking you to either put it away somewhere or at least put it out of sight."

Longarm gave the woman a hard glare, then turned his attention away without answering her.

"If you do not do as I ask," she threatened, "I shall call a policeman."

He looked at the busybody again. "First off, Julesburg don't have policemen. Here they're constables. An' secondly, there's nothing illegal about a man packing iron. In fact it's downright sensible. A man never knows when he might have t'shoot somebody," he added, looking her up and down.

The woman looked like she might have a heart attack. Or shit her drawers. Longarm voted for shitting her drawers, as that was something she would find much more mortifying than the heart attack.

He looked away again and contemplated taking his Colt out and cleaning it or something. But that would be unkind. He ignored her, and eventually she got tired of glaring at him and returned to her own bench and her children.

Chapter 4

"Cheyenne. Everybody out for Cheyenne." The conductor swayed from side to side as he came down the aisle from one coach to the next. "We won't be stopping any longer than to take on freight and westbound passengers, so if you want to disembark, don't dawdle or you'll be in Medicine Bow."

The train stopped and Longarm grabbed his bag. He had to wait for the same snotty female and her brood to clear the steps before he could get off.

"Thanks for the ride," he said with a grin as he stepped foot on the Cheyenne platform.

"Any time. And I mean that sincerely," the conductor said, laughing.

Longarm paused to light a cheroot. He needed to speak with the express agent in Medicine Bow, but he wanted to talk with the Cheyenne agent first to see if they had identified the mailbag, or bags, that had been stolen.

In front of him the woman with the two kids was in negotiation with a hack driver about something. Longarm did not care enough about that conversation to try to listen in on it.

He was about to head for the Union Pacific offices when he heard an angry shout.

"You bitch!" A fat man wearing a derby and boiled shirt was advancing from the far end of the platform.

The woman with the children turned pale as a freshly ironed sheet and grabbed both kids to her as if trying to hide them in the folds of her voluminous skirts.

Longarm was definitely paying attention now.

"Harold," she squeaked in a shaky voice. "Don't."

"You traitorous bitch," Harold bellowed. "Trying to take my boys. You won't get away with any such of a thing."

He was within twenty feet of the woman now. He reached into a pocket and produced a small, nickel-plated revolver. Small, Longarm realized, but certainly lethal. Hell, pip-squeak little .22 rimfires had probably taken more game than every .44-40 ever made, and the puny little things were used to fell steers in abattoirs; there was just no cartridge that would not kill.

The woman began to cry.

"Give me my boys," Harold bawled, "or so help me God I will kill you right where you stand." He stopped and aimed his pistol at her. "Now, send them to me, Margaret, or I'll kill you and them too."

"No, please." Her tears were coming hot and heavy, and now the children were bawling as well. "Don't shoot them, Harold. Please."

"I'm going to shoot you, Margaret. On the count of three. One . . . two . . ."

Harold did not have a chance to say "three" as just before that count a .45 slug blew the right side of his head out into the streets of Cheyenne. A fine red mist hung in the air beside him for several seconds before dissipating on the faint breeze. By that time what was left of Harold had collapsed onto the planks of the U.P. platform, his little revolver clattering onto the ground beside him.

Margaret looked like she would collapse as well. But not so permanently if she did drop.

Longarm shoved his .45 back into its leather and hurried

to her side, but she had hold of her boys and seemed to be recovering by then. For their sake, he supposed, which was as good a reason as any and better than most.

"Sorry the kids had t'see that," he said as he took her elbow to steady her.

"I didn't . . . I don't . . . I mean . . ."

Longarm gave her a smile and said, "Anyhow it's cheaper than a divorce an' a whole lot quicker."

She gave him a stricken look and said, "How could you make light of this. You've taken a life. Don't you even care?"

Longarm frowned right back at her. "Hell, yes, I care. I care that you an' these boys o' yours are alive right now. I care that that man didn't shoot the bunch o' you. Now, if you'll excuse me, lady," he touched the brim of his Stetson and took two steps back from her, "I want t'be shut o' you and this whole damn thing."

The older boy was looking at him with something akin to worship, and Longarm suspected that one did not share his mother's views about the evils of firearms. Longarm looked down and winked at the kid, then spun around and headed for the U.P. offices. He had work to do here.

Chapter 5

A Cheyenne cop caught up with him in the freight agent's office. "Two bags," the express agent was saying. "We identified them as two mailbags that came on in Omaha and were checked through to San Francisco. Of course we have no idea what might have been in either of them."

"Something mighty damn valuable is my guess," Longarm said.

The agent smiled. "You really went out on a limb with that one, Marshal."

That was when the cop intruded on the conversation. "You! You're the one who shot that man, aren't you?" He glared at Longarm and gave him a nervous look, his hand wrapped around the grips of his revolver but the weapon still in its holster.

Longarm looked at him and snorted. "Son, if you really think you're gonna need that shooter, in the leather is *not* the best place t'be havin' it."

"But . . ."

"Yes, sonny," the cop looked like he was not yet old enough to shave, "I'm the one as shot that man. Did it before he could commit murder out there."

"Put your hands up," the cop insisted.

Longarm shrugged and lifted his hands well clear of the Colt on his belt. The Cheyenne policeman still did not have his revolver in his hand though. "You know, don't you, that I coulda emptied my gun in you by now an' had time to reload afterward."

"Huh?" He did, however belatedly, take his revolver out.

"You got a lot to learn, boy. I hope you live long enough to do it," Longarm told him.

"I don't know what you are talking about, sir," the young, blond, rather nervous cop said.

"My point exactly," Longarm told him. He turned to the express agent and said, "Excuse me for a minute, please, while I see what this boy wants." Then he turned back to face the policeman, hands still in the air. "My arms are gettin' tired, son, and while they're up high I can't get at my wallet to show you my badge."

"Badge?"

"You know. Badge. One o' them things that peace officers carry."

"You are . . . ?"

"Deputy United States Marshal Custis Long," Longarm said.

"Oh, I . . . I'm sorry."

"Don't be. Can I put my hands down now?"

"Yes, of course."

Longarm dropped his hands and hooked his thumbs behind his belt buckle immediately, beside his .45. He shook his head and said, "Boy, you shouldn't ought to take somebody's word for somethin' like that. It's so easy for a man to lie, and that sort of lie is the kind that could get you dead if you believe the wrong man. I could be the baddest son of a bitch in the territory and lie to you about bein' a lawman. Make sure of such things before you take a man's word."

"But you said . . ."

"Right. I *said*. But I didn't *show*. As it happens, I really am a deputy marshal, but you *still* don't know that for your own self." He reached inside his coat and pulled out his wallet, flopped it open to display the badge, and said, "*Now* you know. Now you've seen. Now it's safe for you to believe."

The youngster stuffed his pistol back into the leather pouch on his belt, removed his billed cap, and wiped his forehead.

"Haven't faced down many bad men yet, have you?" Longarm observed.

"Oh, drunks and vagrants and pistol-happy cowhands," the cop said. "The usual. But no, uh, no murderers."

"Which I ain't, lucky enough for you," Longarm told him. "Did that woman tell you what happened out there?"

"Woman? What woman?"

"Shit," Longarm mumbled. "All right then. Come over here an' set on this bench. I'll go over the whole thing, and when I'm done here I'll go with you to the police station and make out a statement for your records."

"Thank you. Thank you, sir," the cop said.

"This could take a spell," Longarm said to the Union Pacific's express agent. "Will you still be here?"

"As long as it takes," the man said. "Normal business hours don't apply to something like this, so I will be here whenever you get back."

Longarm nodded and took the young policeman by the arm. "Come along now and we'll get this done, you an' me."

Chapter 6

By the time he was finished at the Cheyenne police station, with their voluminous reports and statements—most of them having to do with the missing intended victim and her two sons—it was six-thirty and the shops up and down the main drag were closing for the night. The express agent was still in his office adjacent to the railroad depot however.

"Sorry to take so long," Longarm said, greeting the agent, whose name was Thomas Harper, and nodding to a slightly younger man who was also there.

"Longarm, this is our night man, Dewey Brannen."

Longarm howdied Brannen and shook hands with the man.

"Dewey is in charge from six P.M. until six A.M. He's the one who handled the mailbags the other night."

"I did, sir," Brannen said. "One bag off for our post office here and two bags on, one going to Salt Lake City and the other to San Francisco. There was also a parcel going to Evanston."

"And everything seemed normal with the onboard agent?"

Brannen nodded. "His name was Farley Oakes."

"He was the regular agent?"

Another nod. "Regular as clockwork."

"Do you know anything about the man?" Longarm asked.

"Not really. He was a good bit older than me, and if we had anything in common we didn't gab enough to find out about that. The passenger trains only stop for a few minutes, so there isn't much time for chatter anyway. Anything that will be here longer, like a freight loading or unloading, we put them on a siding so the main line stays clear. But the thirty-four passenger was routine."

"Do you know where Oakes lived?" Longarm was thinking the agent might well have been in collusion with the robbers, might even have been a participant. After all, he did open the door despite instruction to the contrary.

"I'm not sure. Evanston maybe. That is the next section point on the line. Most of the crew live there. They run east to Omaha, turn around, and run back west. There is a change of train crews in Evanston. I'm not sure, but I had the impression that Oakes lived there too, just like the regular train crew."

"But he was alive and well and acting normal," Longarm said.

"As normal as Oakes got. He wasn't ever very talkative. Like I said, he was a much older man than me."

"All right, thanks." Longarm thought for a moment, then said, "Your next westbound is at twelve-twenty again?"

Harper shook his head. "We have a freight string coming through in," he looked at his watch, "in eight minutes, and a passenger at ten-ten. You don't want to know about the eastbounds?"

"No need," Longarm said. "Not right now anyway. This freight train, though. Will it stop in Medicine Bow?"

"Only if you want it to, Marshal."

Longarm pondered that and said, "I want it to."

"I'll have our station manager make out the order, sir."

"You've been real helpful. Thanks." Longarm retrieved his bag and settled down to wait for his ride to Medicine Bow.

He wondered what had happened to the woman named Margaret, though, and to her two boys. It had been an ugly thing that those boys saw done to their daddy. Longarm regretted hell out of that, but he had not seen that he had any choice about it. The father had been dead serious about killing Margaret and the boys, so it was better they see their father shot down than to be murdered themselves.

Any way you looked at it, though, it was a lousy situation, Longarm thought.

He considered whether he had time to get a drink before the westbound freight arrived. Or a meal. Damn, but he was hungry. And thirsty. The free lunch spread at a friendly tavern would come in awfully handy.

He looked at his watch and decided he would just have to settle for a cheroot, so he pulled one out, bit the twist off, and struck a lucifer to fire it up.

Chapter 7

"I don't suppose there is a café nearby where I could grab a sandwich or something before that freight pulls in," Longarm said to Thomas Harper.

Harper shook his head. "There's a couple of places within a block, block and a half, but at this hour they would be pretty busy. I doubt they could prepare anything for you in time for you to make that train, and we really can't hold it for you. It will only stop for a minute or so to throw off any mail they might be carrying and snatch any train orders, then they are off to California."

"Damn," Longarm mumbled quietly.

"Sir?" It was the night man Brannen.

"Yes, Dewey?"

"If you are hungry . . ."

"Hungry as a damn bear comin' out of hibernation," Longarm said.

The young man pulled open a desk drawer and brought out a small basket that was covered with a red and white checkered cloth. "My ma fixed this up for my supper tonight, Marshal. You can take this and eat it between here and Medicine Bow."

"I don't want to take your supper, son."

"Please do," the young express agent protested. "I'll have plenty of time to walk over to George Dyal's café and get a sit-down meal. George makes great steaks and the best dried apple pie you ever put a tooth to. I'd enjoy getting something over there for a change."

Longarm accepted the basket but reached into his pocket and brought out a Mexican silver peso, as good as a silver dollar anywhere above or below the Rio Grande. "Thanks, Dewey, but only if you let me buy you that dinner at the café."

Brannen grinned. "That's a deal, Marshal. One thing though."

Longarm raised an eyebrow and nodded.

"If you can . . . I know it might not be possible . . . but if you can, would you please send my mom's basket back?"

"I'll do that for sure," Longarm promised. "Count on it."

He hooked the basket over his arm and barely had time to enjoy his cheroot before the westbound freight came to a squealing, hissing, snorting halt beside the platform.

Harper escorted Longarm to the cab and introduced him to the Number 48's engineer.

"Marshal Long here needs a ride to Medicine Bow," Harper said. "Here's your train order for a stop there to let him off."

The engineer did not seem especially pleased with the news, but he grunted, inclined his head toward the fold-down steel jump seat at the back of the big steam engine, and said, "Sit there. Stay out of the way. We'll not be stopping again 'tween here and Medicine Bow."

Longarm nodded. "I'll try to stay out of your way."

"Good. See that you do."

Longarm told Harper good-bye and took his seat before removing the checkered napkin from his lunch basket and digging into the sumptuous meal Mrs. Brannen had prepared for her son Dewey.

Chapter 8

Medicine Bow after dark was not impressive. But then Medicine Bow in broad daylight was less than impressive. Longarm had been there before. Oddly enough, he really liked the place. What it lacked in urban sophistication it made up for in friendliness.

The surly U.P. engineer stopped barely long enough for Longarm to step down onto the platform, then powered away with a gush of steam and a spray of hot cinders from the firebox. The train had not cleared the depot before Longarm remembered Mrs. Brannen's wicker basket, which he had placed underneath his stool aboard the steam engine. The basket was still right there.

"Dammit!" he growled aloud.

"Pardon me?" The speaker was a man of middling height with a carefully trimmed mustache and spectacles that gleamed blankly in the light from the lamps burning on the U.P. platform.

"Sorry," Longarm said, extending his hand and introducing himself.

The fellow smiled, revealing one gold tooth in the center of his upper teeth. "Oh, I know who you are. The telegraphic message from Cheyenne accompanying the train orders told me that. I'm Chet Powers." His smile broadened. "Night express agent, telegrapher, station manager, and general dogsbody for all needs."

"Good," Longarm said. "You're the man I need to see about the robbery the other night."

"Yes, sir, so I am," Powers said.

"First, though, I got a favor to ask of you in your telegrapher capacity."

"Sure, whatever you need."

"I left something aboard that engine and I'd like it returned."

Powers said, "Name it. I can wire ahead to them. The next scheduled stop is Rock Springs to take on water, but if you like I can have the Rawlins station lay a torpedo and hang a message bag for you."

"That might be the ticket," Longarm said. He explained about Mrs. Brannen's prized basket.

Powers laughed and said, "We wouldn't want Dewey to get in trouble with his mama. I'll wire that to them, then you and me can sit down and talk about the robbery. Not that there is so very much that I can tell you, but I'll do whatever you ask."

"Thanks. You do that. In the meantime I'm gonna walk over to that saloon that I see across the way. Those lights are callin' me and I just can't resist. Come join me when you get that message off an' I'll buy you a drink or two whilst I pick your brain."

"I wish I could do that, Marshal, but I have to stay here close to my key in case there is message traffic moving."

"All right then, Chet, I'll go get me a drink or two an' come back here for our talk. How's that?"

Powers's smile flashed again. "That sounds fine to me, Marshal."

Longarm deposited his carpetbag beside the depot door and excused himself, his thirst growing every step of the way across an open square to the Blue Dog Saloon.

Chapter 9

Longarm thought he was about as close to heaven as he was ever apt to get. The beer they had on tap at the Blue Dog was dark and heavy and delightful, brought in by rail from Chicago fresh and tasty and crisp on the tongue.

"Now if only you have a good rye whiskey," Longarm said to the bartender, whose name, Jim, was written on the bib of his apron along with a caricature of a sad-eyed dog.

Jim smiled and said, "I have some Rock Hill rye, Maryland distilled and smooth as springwater."

"Jim, you have made me a happy man tonight," Longarm told him. "I'll have a wee glass of that good stuff. And that bowl of peanuts if I may."

The rye was even better than Jim had suggested, so Longarm had two.

"Another?"

Longarm shook his head. "Thanks, but I'm working. Say, you could do me a favor though, if you would."

"If I can, sure," the friendly bartender said.

"I'm needin' a place to sleep tonight. Is there a hotel in town? There wasn't none the last time I was here."

It was Jim's turn to shake his head sadly. "Sorry, friend, but there still isn't." He turned and addressed the handful of other men who were lined up along the bar. "Anybody know of anyone open to take in a boarder for a night or two?"

The only response that drew was a suggestion by one man to "Try Bertie. The regular places are both full up right now."

"Bertie?" Longarm asked.

Jim chuckled. "Bertie is Miss Bertha Bidwell. She hasn't lived here long, but she has become what you might call a local institution."

"You think she might have room for me?"

Jim grinned hugely. "I'm positive she would."

"Might she open the door to a stranger at this hour?"

"Yes, indeed. I promise it. Bertie is open all night, every night," Jim said, a comment that drew some laughter from the other end of the bar.

Longarm finally caught on. "Miss Bertha Bidwell runs a whorehouse."

The laughter increased. "Yes, but you won't find a finer one anyplace this side of San Francisco."

"If that's my only option . . ." Longarm said.

"It is."

"Then give me directions to it," Longarm told him. "I'll head over there after I get my business done."

Chapter 10

"You should understand that the 34 train serves a quarter of the country. More, really," Chet Powers, the Medicine Bow station agent, said, gesturing with one upturned palm as if showing what he meant on a map, even though there was no map hanging in front of him. "It runs clear through from Omaha to San Francisco. Carries mail for the whole of the northern plains, the Rocky Mountains, the high desert, northwest and northern California. All of that."

Powers paused to take a swallow of steaming hot coffee, then went on to say, "Mail is brought over by riverboat and ferry from the entire East and collected in Omaha. Because there is so much of it, the 34 has a separate mail car, not just a corner of the baggage car like on shorter-run trains.

"It wouldn't be so difficult to rob the mail from a baggage car. Passengers have the right to reach their luggage en route, so those cars are never locked. But the dedicated mail cars always are," Powers said, emphasizing "always."

"When that car reached us, the usual thing was for me to call out and then Oakes would open up for me. We would exchange mailbags if necessary and then he would lock up again."

"And this time?" Longarm asked.

"This time the door was standing open a couple inches. I could see right off that it was unlocked. Naturally I signaled to the engineer to lay off. I climbed in. Oakes was facedown on the floor. There was an awful lot of blood." Powers grimaced. "Marshal, I have to tell you, I didn't realize one man could bleed so awful much. I'd rather I didn't know it now."

"I know what you mean," Longarm said. There had been a time when he did not possess that particular bit of information, but that was long in the past.

"How was he shot? Do you know?" he asked.

Powers said, "I didn't look all that close. I'm sure he was shot in the back of the head. If there were any other wounds," he shrugged, "I just didn't get down and look."

"What about the body?" Longarm asked.

"I wired for instructions. The body went on to Evanston, just like it was. We didn't try to clean the blood or anything. Because the car was dedicated to mail carriage, I did inventory the mail. There is a running log, you see, to show what comes on and where it goes and what goes off. It didn't take long to see that two bags were missing."

"Exactly two?"

Powers nodded. "Right. They both came on at Omaha. Past that, though, I couldn't tell from the log."

"And they were going where?"

"On through to San Francisco, both of them."

"Were there other bags headed there?"

"No, sir. Those were the only two on that train."

"What about the safe?" Longarm asked. "Mail cars have safes, don't they?"

"They do, but this one was secure."

"Could Oakes have opened the safe if the robbers tried to force him to help?" Longarm was thinking perhaps the mail agent refused to cooperate and that was why he was murdered.

"Yes, sir," Powers said with a nod and a swallow of his

coffee. "The key to the safe was in his pocket. Doc Anderson found that when he was checking the man over."

"Anderson?" Longarm asked. "Who's he?"

"Local man. Pretty good doctor. He won't be awake at this hour, but if you want him right now . . ."

"No, he can wait until morning." Longarm stifled a yawn and thought about asking Powers for a cup of that coffee. On the other hand, he did not want to do anything that would keep him awake.

He grunted softly while he continued his thought process. Oakes could have resisted opening the safe, but if that were so, the robbers could have taken the key out of his pocket after they killed him, and they hadn't. That idea would seem to be a dead end.

Two mailbags were taken, both of them brought aboard in Omaha and destined for San Francisco.

"So whoever it was took all the mail taken aboard in Omaha and headed for San Francisco."

"Exactly," Powers said. He paused, hesitant about something, then said, "Are we going to be in trouble about this? I mean, is the Union Pacific likely to lose our mail franchise because of it?"

"I wouldn't think so. Not that it's any of my never mind," Longarm told him. "Hell, even if that was an issue, your job would be safe here, as much as you do."

Powers laughed. "Last Christmas I bought a few shares of stock in the company. I wouldn't want to see them go down in value. They likely would if we lost the postal contract. That brings in good money, or so I'm told."

"That explains it," Longarm said with a smile. It had occurred to him, and not just now, that Chet Powers would have had an opportunity to enter the mail car and kill Oakes. Of course then he would have had the problem of hiding two mailbags before any of the train crew responded to his signal stopping the train where it was.

Besides, in Longarm's opinion Powers was not the sort

to commit murder or theft either one. He quickly discarded that theory.

"You say the body went on to Evanston?"

"Yes, sir. That is what the section boss told me to do."

"All right. I'll check with them later. Right now I think I'd better get some sleep." He picked up the carpetbag he had left at the depot and said, "Thanks for your help, Chet. I may have more questions later."

"Any time, Marshal. If there is any way I can help . . ." He spread his hands, then picked up his coffee cup again. "Our day man, Gordon Rahl, will be on duty tomorrow, but if you need me, he can show you how to find me."

"Thanks, Chet. Good night."

Chapter 11

Bertie Bidwell's whorehouse was a two-story affair, something of a rarity in little Medicine Bow. About half the houses in the town were shotgun affairs, one or sometimes two old railroad cars fitted end to end with a one-hole shithouse dug nearby and water carried from the town well beside the railroad tracks. That one well supplied most of the needs of the community, in addition to providing for the replenishment of the thirsty U.P. steam engines.

An oversized red lantern hung by the front door, honoring what had become a trademark of whorehouses across the country. That all started when railroad crews would come off duty and head for the nearest piece of ass, carrying their red signal lanterns with them, hanging the lanterns outside when they went indoors to see what was on offer.

In Bertie's case, Longarm got a huge surprise.

He knocked on the door and was quickly admitted. But the place was not at all what he was expecting.

In a small town like Medicine Bow he was expecting a shabby place with a handful of worn-out girls who would screw for fifty cents or go half and half for another quarter.

Instead he walked into a setting that could have been

mistaken for the finest house of gentlemanly pleasure in New Orleans or Chicago.

The foyer and the parlor were large, quiet, and sumptuously furnished. Not in garish red tones either, but in muted shades of blue and gold.

The paintings on the walls were of landscapes, bucolic scenes. There was not a nude anywhere in sight. Longarm suspected these had been painted by top-flight artists, although he did not bother examining them for signatures. Even if he saw a famous artist's name, he probably would not recognize it.

The best part of it all, however, was the lady who opened the door.

And Custis Long was not a man to throw the term "lady" around willy-nilly.

This one was . . . a lady. No doubt about it. One look was all it took.

"You're Bertie?"

She nodded, a very slight dip of her chin. That was all. But a faint hint of a smile played on lips that were red. A subtle red, however, nothing garish. The hue appeared to be natural and not some artificial coloring.

Bertie Bidwell was tall, almost meeting Longarm eye to eye as she stood there in high heels. Slender as a knife blade. If she had tits, which he supposed that she must, they were well hidden by the modest gown she wore. There was no need to guess about her waist, however. It was tiny. Surely it would not really be possible for his two hands to reach around that waist and touch at the back . . . but he would almost have sworn that he could.

Her butt, and again she was certain to have one, was as well hidden as her tits.

Her face was long and narrow, her neck slender and patrician. Her cheekbones were high, her eyebrows thin—he guessed that she surely must pluck them to keep them so— and her eyes were a soft, almost golden brown. Her hair was a deep, gleaming black. It was pinned high and held at the back by a chignon that exactly matched its shade and luster.

The gown was silk in a pale, dusty blue shade that went very well with the décor of the parlor.

Longarm suspected that this woman was . . . special. He wondered what the hell she was doing running a whorehouse in Medicine Bow, Wyoming Territory.

No, he thought, not just running it. He felt certain she would be the owner of this classy establishment.

Bertie Bidwell, he suspected, was very much her own woman.

He coughed into his fist, feeling suddenly almost shy here.

She smiled, purely angelic, and asked, "And what specialty would you prefer, sir?"

"What, uh, specialty?" he repeated.

That smile appeared again. "We have ladies who can provide almost any service you require."

"Ah, yes," he said, finally understanding. No, this was not some fuck-and-good-bye outfit. And in a flash of comprehension he asked, "Where do your, uh, customers come from, Miss Bidwell?"

"Please call me Bertie. To answer your question, our patrons come from everywhere the Union Pacific reaches. Many come specifically to visit our happy little house."

"Y'know," he said, "I'm bettin' they come just t'visit you, Bertie."

The smile. Lordy, he did like that smile. "You still have not told me what you require this evening."

Longarm laughed and introduced himself. "What I'm lookin' for, Bertie, is a good night's sleep. There's no hotel, and the boardinghouses are full up, so either I hire a room from you for the night or I walk over to the livery an' sleep in the straw."

"You see, I'm a deputy United States marshal, and if you let me stay here, I'll be paying you with a voucher drawn on the treasury of that same United States."

Bertie chuckled, her fine-boned shoulders rising and falling as she did so. "That, Deputy, would be a first. Do you mean to say that the government of the United States would pay for a night in a house of ill repute?"

Longarm grinned. "Yes'm, that's exactly what I'm sayin'."

"Then, Deputy, you are most welcome. Would you like a drink before I escort you to your room?"

"That sounds mighty nice," he said, following Bertie into the parlor, where two well-dressed gentlemen were being served drinks by a stunning redhead with magnificent tits and bright green eye shadow.

It must be awfully nice, Longarm thought, to be a rich man. It was something he would never know. But for this little while he could live like one.

"What is your pleasure?" the redhead asked in a sultry voice. He was not at all sure she was talking about drinks, but for the moment that would have to do.

Chapter 12

The room Bertie gave him was huge. It was decorated in rose tones, very feminine as to both appearance and the perfumed scent that filled the space. Drapes were drawn decorously over the two windows on the outside corner walls. The floor was covered almost wall to wall by an ivory rug with a complex pattern of roses woven into it. He felt almost reluctant to walk on such a rug with his much-traveled boots.

He thought about that, and then, feeling a mite foolish, except there was no one there to witness his silliness, he removed the boots before walking into the room.

Longarm carried his boots and his carpetbag to a low luggage bench below one of the windows, then set the boots beneath the bench and his bag onto it. He quickly stripped, hanging his things on a clothes tree, splashed a little water from a pitcher into the basin that sat on a small table, and with a washcloth lying nearby wiped away some of the day's sweat and grime.

He was feeling infinitely better when he turned down the covers on the big four-poster and slid between the sheets.

There is nothing, he thought, quite so cool and comforting as silk sheets and a pillow covered in silk to accompany those sheets.

Before he could finish the thought, he dropped into a sound sleep.

Longarm already had his Colt in hand and was sitting up in the bed before he came fully awake. He did not know what the hell had woken him up, but . . . he felt a flush of heat rise in his cheeks. *There was a ghost standing by the door.*

The wraith was slender and pale and dimly seen in the dark of the room. It was . . .

"Did I wake you, Marshal?"

It was Bertie standing there, that's what it was.

"Woke me an' scared the shit outta me," he confessed, pushing the .45 back into its leather. He heard her chuckle.

"I'm sorry."

"You don't sound real sorry."

"No, but it is the polite thing to say, is it not?" The chuckle became a laugh. "The truth is that I came in here fully intending to wake you."

Longarm lay back on the bed. It was still comfortable, but the silk sheets were no longer as cool as when he first lay on them.

"Now that you are awake, I suppose the proper thing would be to ask you . . . may I join you?"

"Here?"

"Yes, of course. Where else?"

"I just . . . uh . . . reckon I don't know hardly what t'say. Except for you to come on in here. You're mighty welcome. What time is it?"

"It will soon be dawn. My customers have all gone home to their wives, or else they are sleeping peacefully in their rooms. I've locked the front door and extinguished the lanterns, and now I need to get some sleep myself."

"This is your own room?" he asked.

Bertie sat on the edge of the bed, her weight so slight that he scarcely felt the shift of the mattress. He could see now that she was not wearing a pale gown. The fact was that she was wearing nothing at all.

"Would you mind . . . ?"

"What?"

He did not answer. He leaned over, struck a match, and lighted the lamp that was on the bedside table, beside his coiled gunbelt and revolver. He turned to Bertie and smiled. "The better to see you, ma'am."

And seeing her was a very good thing indeed.

Bertie was slim as a reed. Pale and perfect, her tits—yes, she did have two—were like tea saucers fashioned of bone china, the nipples small and pink. Her waist was as tiny as he'd thought and her butt tidy and shapely. She was so slender that he could see her ribs beneath the skin. Her belly button was an outy. Her pussy hair had been shaved so that her mound was completely bald.

"May I say that I like what I see," he said.

Bertie smiled back at him. "Then would you do me the favor of throwing that sheet aside so I can see what you have under there."

Longarm's smile turned to a grin.

He swept the silk sheet away and held out his arms to Bertie Bidwell.

Chapter 13

"You feel good there," he said. "You fit against me just fine."

Bertie murmured something he did not hear, her mouth being occupied with his right nipple.

"Damn, that feels good," he said as he stroked her hair and the back of her head. He ran his fingers down her spine, played with her butt for a moment, and smoothed her hair down. She was such a pleasure that he did not know where to stop. More to the point, he did not want to stop at all. He wanted to feel her, all of her.

Bertie ran the tip of her tongue around his nipple and nipped it lightly with her lips and then, very gently, with her teeth. "Do you like that?"

"Mmm."

She laughed. "I know something you will like even better." She slid down to his waist, her tongue moving over his flesh as she did so. And then beyond.

She found the hot, throbbing pole of his erection and licked that too. She peeled his foreskin back and ran her tongue around the hard bulb of his glans; licked briefly at the hole in the end, then took the head of his cock into the warmth of her mouth.

Longarm arched his back, lifting his prick to her. Bertie sucked hard on him, drawing him deep into her mouth.

"That feels . . . Oh, damn, that's good, it . . ." Without warning he felt the sudden rise of his cum as he exploded into her mouth.

Bertie stayed with him there, continuing to suckle until he had finished.

"Sorry," he said. "I didn't know that was comin'."

"And come it did," she agreed, sounding pleased with herself. "Your cum tastes good, by the way. Very sweet and nice. I like it."

"Why, ma'am, you can have all of it that you're of a mind to harvest."

She laughed again. "I like you, Custis Long."

"Why thank you, Miz Bidwell. Fact o' the matter is, I like you pretty good too."

She retraced her route up the length of his body and nestled into the crook of his shoulder.

Longarm ran a hand up and down her body, finding that her tits were firm and her nipples hard as diamonds. He bent his head and sucked on her left nipple for a moment, then slipped a hand between her legs.

Her pussy was wet and welcoming. He slid a finger in two knuckles deep, brought it back out a bit, and felt for the tiny button of her pleasure. When he found that and began gently stroking it, Bertie's head lolled back and her eyes closed.

"Nice," she whispered. "So nice. Would you mind finishing me there? Just a . . . I can feel it . . . Oh. Oh!"

He felt her body shudder with wave after wave of pleasure as she reached her own climax. Then she sank back on the mattress with a long, happy sigh. "Nice," she said again.

Longarm kissed her then, erect once more, and raised himself above Bertie's pale, slender form. He levered her legs apart and pushed between them. Bertie reached down to find and guide him in, and he sank deep into her flesh. He felt her gasp at his size as he entered, but she quickly accommodated his entry. Her hips began to rise to his first slow thrusts, then soon they found their mutual rhythm and the pace intensified, until he was driving hard and deep, their bellies slapping wetly together with every stroke.

Bertie cried out again, loud this time, and collapsed exhausted onto the silk sheets.

Longarm braced himself over her as he too reached a climax, his cum spewing deep inside Bertie's slim body.

He kissed her and with a grin muttered, "I been woke up worse ways than that."

She smiled. "Hush up now. I need to get some sleep. So do you."

Longarm rolled off of the lovely woman, closed his eyes, and was almost immediately asleep again.

Chapter 14

Longarm woke with Bertie's face inches in front of his. She was still sleeping soundly. He smiled and pulled away, rolling over to the edge of the four-poster and getting up as quietly as he could lest he wake her.

He padded naked and barefoot to the washstand. The basin held a few inches of tepid water with a washcloth floating in it. He wrung some of the water out and used the washcloth to clean the dried cum and pussy juice from his cock, then silently dressed. He was pulling his boots on, when he heard, "Good morning, Custis."

"Did I wake you? Sorry."

"No, it's time for me to get up anyway. I have to make out a grocery list, run errands, all manner of things. I can't lie here all day long." She smiled. "But I would like to if you were in bed with me. I enjoyed this morning."

"So did I," he admitted.

"Would you like some more? It wouldn't take long."

"I'd love to," he said, "but I have work to do."

"Then at least join me for breakfast. You have to eat regardless, and it might as well be here."

"Sounds fine," he said.

Bertie shoved the covers back and stood, her slender body

pale and beautiful. She took a light blue silk dressing gown from behind a modesty screen in a corner of the room and belted it around herself, then led the way downstairs and to the kitchen at the back of the big house.

An elderly black woman was already there and had a good fire going in the ornate cast iron and chromium stove. Longarm assumed she was the cook, or perhaps a servant of some capacity.

"Good morning, Mama," Bertie said, kissing the woman on the cheek. She turned to Longarm and said, "Custis, this is my mother, Antoinette Bidwell. Mama, this is Deputy Custis Long."

Antoinette gave Longarm a suspicious look. "You be careful of my baby's heart, boy."

"Yes, ma'am." Longarm suddenly felt as if he had been caught doing something he should not. It was silly for him to feel that way, he knew. But he felt it nonetheless.

"Toast and an omelet?" Bertie asked.

"What?"

She repeated the question and he nodded. "Sure. D'you happen t'have coffee too?"

"Of course." Bertie rose onto her tiptoes and kissed Longarm. He liked the kiss but was very conscious of Antoinette looking disapprovingly on them. "Mama, is the coffee ready?"

Antoinette nodded curtly, and Bertie fetched two china cups from a cabinet and filled them, giving one to Longarm and taking the other to a place at the head of a long table. "Mama will have breakfast ready in a few minutes," she said.

Longarm sat. He supposed the food when it came was good, but he could not say that he enjoyed it much. He was all too aware of Antoinette's disapproval. But then the woman surely knew where he had spent the night. And what he had been doing with Bertie. It was an awkward feeling and rare.

He ate mechanically, head down and barely responding

to Bertie's attempts at conversation. As soon as he finished breakfast, he excused himself from the table.

Bertie went with him to the front door and gave him a long kiss good-bye. Longarm, however, was looking past her to the kitchen door, where Antoinette's disapproving stare was willing daggers at him.

"Come back tonight," Bertie whispered in a husky voice.

"If I can," he said, not meaning a word of it. He stepped outside into what proved to be afternoon sunlight, jammed his hat on, and headed for the Union Pacific depot.

Chapter 15

The day man, Gordon Rahl, was on duty in the U.P. office.
"Anything for me?" Longarm asked.

Rahl shook his head. "Nothing, marshal."

"Where can I find Powers at this time o' day then?
There's some things I still need to ask him."

"Chet lives just this side of the livery. Do you know
where that is?"

Longarm nodded. "Saw that yesterday."

"Chet's place is the second house this side. It's on the
south side of the street. In the front yard close by the fence
there's an old washtub filled with dirt and a lot of red flowers of some kind. You can't miss it."

Longarm sometimes wondered why practically everyone
who gave a man directions thought he had to end with "you
can't miss it," when quite often you could indeed miss the
desired destination. And without even having to work at it.
"Thanks. I'll go see if he's in."

"Oh, he'll be in. Probably awake by now, but knock light
on the door in case he's not. His wife will hear and open it
for you if Chet is still sleeping."

"I'll do that," Longarm said.

He easily found the house with the white painted rail

fence in front and the old washtub being used as a planter for red . . . like Gordon Rahl, he was not exactly sure just what the red flowers were, but whatever they were they were a nice touch of color.

He stepped up onto the front porch and very lightly tapped on the door. After a few moments he heard footsteps approaching, then the door was opened by a young woman— a girl, really—with pale blond hair and bright blue eyes. She had her hair up in a bun and had a smudge of flour on her left cheek.

Longarm snatched his hat off. "Mrs. Powers?"

"Yes," she said hesitantly.

Longarm introduced himself, and her obvious skepticism evaporated. She smiled and said, "Chet told me about you, Marshal. Come in, please. Can I get you something?"

"I'm fine, ma'am, but I do want t'speak with Chet again. Will he be getting up soon, d'you think?"

"I can wake him now. It is almost time for him to get up anyway."

"That'd be fine, thanks."

"Won't you come inside? I can give you a cup of coffee while Chet gets himself around."

"You're mighty nice." He followed the young woman through an overfurnished little house to the tiny kitchen tacked onto the back, where she gave him a mug of hot coffee and disappeared into another part of the house. Longarm was halfway through the coffee when Chet came out, bleary eyed, stuffing his shirttail into his trousers.

"What can I do for you, Longarm?" he asked.

"The passengers that got off the train here that night," Longarm said. "I need to talk with them."

Powers poured coffee for himself and joined Longarm at the somewhat battered kitchen table. He shook his head. "As far as I know there were no passengers that came off here that night. Not from the 34 train anyway."

"None? I thought . . ."

"No, sir, no one. I'm sure of that because Marshal Toler asked the same thing."

"Toler," Longarm said. "He would be . . . ?"

"Part-time town marshal. He's also our blacksmith. John is a good man. Has a place just the other side of the livery." Powers smiled and said, "You can't miss it."

"All right, Chet, thanks. And thank your wife for me, would you."

Powers walked with him to the front door, stopping there and pointing toward the nearby livery. "Just the other side."

"Right. Thanks." Longarm snugged his Stetson onto his head and headed for the smithy.

Chapter 16

John Toler was a hairy man. When Longarm found him, Toler was stoking his forge with fresh coal. He was of medium height and wearing grimy bib overalls beneath a leather apron. His forearms looked like they were probably stronger than the iron he was shaping. He had a full beard and tufts of black hair sticking out of his armpits. He was sweating profusely from the heat coming off the forge.

"Be with you in a minute," Toler said, taking a second to swipe the back of his wrist across his brow.

Longarm nodded and found a seat on the tongue of a manure spreader with a broken wheel spoke. It was a very short wait, then Toler left his forge to come over and apologize.

"What can I do for you?" he asked.

Longarm stood and offered his hand. He introduced himself and said, "I'm here to see you in your marshal capacity."

Toler nodded. "Heard you were in town," he said. "Let me finish welding this hoe, then I'll join you at the Blue Dog for a beer and a snack."

"I'll meet you there, sir."

Longarm had not finished his first beer before the marshal came in, this time without the apron and with a clean denim shirt worn tail out over the overalls. He was not carrying a weapon of any sort, at least none that Longarm could see.

The two got settled at a table with beer and cigars, then Longarm said, "You can prob'ly guess why I'm here."

Toler's expression sobered. "Of course. It's that murder aboard the 34 train the other night."

"Exactly. I'm hoping you know something about it. Anything that will help give me a lead to who did it."

"I wish I could help you, Deputy, but I was sound asleep when Chet found the body. No one told me about it until the next morning. Then Doc Anderson dropped by to talk and he mentioned it." Toler shook his head. "A terrible thing indeed."

"Do you have any idea who might have done it or how?"

"No, none. Doc said it's a mystery to him as well, the car being unlocked and Oakes lying dead on the floor there. To tell you the God's honest truth, I'm pleased the Union Pacific bosses wanted the body taken over to Evanston. That is way out of my jurisdiction, and they are entitled to it for all I care." He took a long pull at his beer and said, "I'm sorry I can't help you, Deputy. If there are any answers, maybe you can find them in Evanston. I'm thinking you won't find them here."

Toler finished his beer and stood. "If you will excuse me, Deputy, I need to get back to my shop."

"Of course. Thanks for your time."

After Toler left, Longarm sat for a while. He had another cheroot and a shot of Jim's excellent rye whiskey, then drained off the rest of his beer and, with a smile, thought perhaps Bertie's doves might possibly have heard something since the murder. That was certainly excuse enough for him to go talk to her about it.

Chapter 17

Longarm ambled out into the twilight. His beer had led to another and perhaps another after that. Now his belly was sour from the pickled sausages he had been munching. What he needed was a proper supper and then that talk with Bertie's girls. He smiled. With Bertie too, for that matter. A *long* talk with Bertie Bidwell.

He was passing the U.P. depot when Chet Powers stepped outside and waved to him. "Marshal. Marshal Long. Yoo-hoo!"

Yoo-hoo? What the hell kind of grown man called "Yoo-hoo"?

The answer to that was obvious enough. Chet did. Longarm altered course and aimed himself in Chet's direction. "What can I do for ya, Chester?"

Chet looked confused. "My name isn't Chester, sir."

"It isn't? I thought . . ."

"My proper name is Chet. Just Chet. It says so in my mama's Bible."

"Sorry. I didn't know that. Now, what can I do for you?"

"I just passed a message through from Doug Baxter in Evanston. The message was going on to Cheyenne, but I thought it was something you ought to know about."

"All right. What is it then?"

"Doug wasn't exactly sure about who has jurisdiction over this robbery and murder, so he thought maybe the fellows in Cheyenne would want to know, sir."

"Know what, Chet?"

"Doug says there is a woman there that might could have something to do with the robber gang, that's what."

Longarm's eyebrows went up and he said, "Tell me more about this woman."

"Doug says this woman is acting real strange. And he says Farley Oakes's widow is hopping mad jealous. Says this woman has been asking personal questions about Oakes. Wanting to know when he'll be buried and stuff like that."

"That seems innocent enough to me."

"Marshal, Doug says this woman is pretending to be some kind of distant relative of Oakes. Except Molly Oakes knows darn good and well that Oakes didn't *have* any relatives. She says this lady is lying through her teeth. Doug added that he doesn't know anything about that, but one thing he does know is that this woman . . . she came through the depot overnight and this morning asked where she could find the Oakes family . . . Doug says if it gave him a crack at this lady, why, *he* would rob the next train himself."

"That's what he said?" Longarm asked.

Chet dropped his gaze toward the toes of his shoes and scuffed the ground a little. "Close enough," he said. "Maybe not exact." He looked up again. "But that's what he meant. I know Doug pretty good and I can tell you true what he was saying."

"Did you save the exact message?"

Chet shook his head. "I receipted for it, passed along the part that was meant for Cheyenne, and burnt the message slip."

"You didn't want to get a friend in trouble, is that it?"

"Yes, sir," Chet said, nodding. "Doug and me are friends.

Have been since we were buttons. We both went to school together and studied telegraphy together too." He gave Longarm a worried look. "Are you gonna peach on me, Marshal?"

"No, no need for that," Longarm said. He thought for a moment and asked, "When did your friend say Oakes will be buried?"

"Tomorrow. Two o'clock," Chet said.

"And this woman will be there?"

Chet shrugged. "She was asking about the burying. Doug figures likely she'll be there, but of course he couldn't say for sure."

Longarm pulled out his Ingersoll and glanced at it. "When will the next train be through?"

"Passenger?"

"Anything on wheels," Longarm told him.

"We have a through freight due by in, um," Powers consulted his watch too, "in thirty-eight minutes."

"Is there time to get a stop order sent to them?" Longarm asked.

"Sure. I could wire down the line and have them lay a torpedo and hang a stop order for you."

"All right. Do it. I want to be on that train and I'll want off again at Evanston. And say, have you heard anything about Mrs. Brannen's basket?"

"No, sir, but I can ask about that too. Anybody up or down the line."

"Thanks. Get those wires off, please, while I go collect my carpetbag an' get ready to spend another miserable damn night on the rails."

"Aw, Marshal, it ain't all that bad, is it?"

Longarm grinned at him. "Helluva lot worse than what I had me in mind for tonight, but it'll have t'do. Go on with you now. I'll be back in a few minutes and join you."

Chet turned and scampered away toward the depot while

Longarm headed out with a very different idea than he'd
originally had.

But, damn, that was another meal he would miss this
time out. He was commencing to feel like his luck was running bad.

Chapter 18

Longarm trotted back to the Blue Dog. He laid down a nickel for a beer he did not really want, then built himself a cheese sandwich with hot mustard. That would have to do for a supper. No pickled sausages this time, though, or any pickled eggs either. Dry, crumbly bread, thick slabs of rat cheese, and a slathering of the mustard and that was supper. He ate it on his way back to the depot. The flavor was nothing special, but it filled the hole in his belly.

"I got your message off, Marshal," Powers told him when he returned to the depot. "They'll stop for you in," he looked at his watch, "in twelve minutes."

"Do me another favor, Chet?"

"Sure, Marshal. Whatever you need."

"When the train stops, give the engineer instructions to stop in Evanston too. I intend to ride in the damn caboose this time. No more o' those steel chairs like they have in the cab."

Chet laughed. "They have to stop in Evanston anyway to take on water and coal, but I'll surely tell them."

"Good. Thanks." Longarm took his carpetbag down the platform toward where he expected the caboose would stop. He waved good-bye to Chet and concentrated on looking for his ride west.

* * *

Evanston was a smoky sprawl. Coal was piled along the tracks in mounds that were higher than most of the roofs in the town. There was even a roundhouse, rare along the U.P., and a huge, handsome depot as well.

He arrived as dawn was breaking behind him. The air was clean and crisply cool. Low clouds scudded overhead. He climbed down from the U.P. freight's caboose, thanked the train crew for their hospitality—they had let him catch some sleep on one of their bunks—and headed for the depot.

Longarm was surprised to see so many Chinese on the streets, until he recalled that there was a joss house here, something to do with Chinese religion, although he did not know just what function that might be.

Apparently the Chinese had come to the west end of Wyoming as laborers on the railroad, started building to meet their own needs, and stayed, or at least frequently visited.

He let himself into the station and asked the young man behind the counter, "Are you Baxter?"

The fellow shook his head. "Doug's off duty. He left, oh, twenty minutes ago or thereabouts."

Longarm grunted. He was not especially disappointed. He could speak with the Evanston telegrapher later. "Do you know Farley Oakes?"

"Did know," the day man corrected him. "Oakes is dead, you know."

"I heard that. Can you tell me where he lived, please?"

"Could. Don't know that I should."

Longarm fashioned a smile that held not the least hint of mirth or of warmth. "You should tell me because, given the mood I am in, son, I may reach across this counter and beat the shit outa you if you don't."

The young man gaped, his mouth falling open and his eyes bugging wide.

"You can also tell me because I am a deputy U.S.

marshal and I just damn well want to know. Now then, would you like any other reasons for you to tell me what I want to know?"

"N-no, sir. Those will do well enough. What you do is, you go out through that door there and turn to your left. You walk down the tracks about two hundred yards and . . ."

The directions seemed simple enough. Longarm very politely thanked the fellow, deposited his carpetbag on the other side of the counter without asking for permission, and headed off to find first a breakfast and second the Oakes residence.

Chapter 19

Longarm found himself procrastinating. He took a room at the Elkhorn Hotel. Went back to the U.P. depot to collect his carpetbag and transfer it to the sparsely furnished hotel room. Surrounded a belly-warming breakfast. Looked up a barbershop and got a shave and a trim—not the mustache, though; he trusted only himself to trim the mustache. Bought a newspaper and sat in the hotel lobby reading it.

By the time all that was done, it was the middle of the morning.

And Mrs. Oakes would see her husband laid to rest at two that afternoon.

It seemed a mighty poor time—and a mighty poor day—to be calling on the woman. Better, perhaps, to at least wait until after the funeral.

Right now the lady was likely swamped with visitors, neighbors bringing food for the wake or whatever sort of service, the Oakes clan, family if there were any here, railroad folk come to support one of their own.

No, he realized, this would be a poor time to approach the widow. Later might work out better.

He finished reading the local paper, bought one from San Francisco and another from New York and read both

of them too—it was remarkable how similar the news sto-
ries were, but then he could attribute that to the telegraph.
News could travel across the entire country in a flash. He
sometimes wondered what news hawks had done in the days
before that telegraphic connection from coast to coast. He
had been only a kid in those days, much too young to care
a fig about news and newspapers and such. Now he enjoyed
them and often found them useful as well.

Longarm sighed, finished his reading, laid both papers
aside so some other traveler could find and enjoy them, and
returned to the café where he had had breakfast. He lounged
over coffee and crullers, then had a light lunch and headed
for the viewing that would precede the funeral service.

Farley Oakes was laid out in the parlor of his little row
house. It was difficult to tell what the man might have looked
like in life. His face was misshapen, probably by the bullet
to the head that had ended his life, and although the undertaker had shaved him, Oakes's face was colored by powders
and eye shadow to the point that it seemed more a mask than
a representation of a living being.

He had been stuffed into a suit that was several sizes too
large for a man who had been rather small. Whoever had
put him in there had not gotten the coat to lie right over the
shoulders, and Longarm kept wanting to tug here and tuck
there so the man would be more comfortable. Which was
ridiculous, of course. Oakes would never know comfort or
any other thing again. Not now that he lay dead in a box
with a lot of sad-faced men and weeping women streaming
through the house.

Flowers were not common in Evanston, not even shipped
in from California, but someone had found a few sprigs of
wild daisies to put in a vase at the head of the coffin, which
sat across two kitchen chairs that no one had bothered trying to disguise.

All in all Longarm found it to be a dreary experience.

But then what could he expect of a solemn funeral for a man he had never known.

He passed through, stared down at the husk of the thing that had been Farley Oakes, then slipped out back to the shitter so he could get rid of some of the coffee he had spent the morning drinking.

He got a good look at the widow, who proved to be a matronly sort with steel gray hair and the obligatory black widow's weeds and light veil. He suspected she weighed twice what Oakes had.

The visitors were mostly railroad men, wearing their Sunday best and with their soft caps clutched nervously in their hands. The ladies were drab, mousy little things. Those would be neighbors and the wives of the railroaders.

There was, however, one glaring exception, and she stood out from the crowd like a Thoroughbred in a pen full of mules. That one was slim and elegant. She was dressed just like the others, in dark clothing unrelieved by jewelry or bright colors, but there was no mistaking that this was a woman of a different stripe. There was something about her, her carriage or the way she held her head, that made her difference known.

That, Longarm suspected, would be the woman whose presence had angered the widow.

Who was it who told him about that? He could not remember. Not that he needed to. He could see it in the way the Widow Oakes looked at this visitor.

Longarm helped himself to some pork chops and potato salad from the groaning sideboard that had been set up on sawhorses in the front yard, and then it was time for the entire gathering to troop along through the streets to the cemetery that lay on the outskirts of town.

There were a few light wagons to carry the ladies the distance.

Again he noticed the lady with the dark auburn hair and the long, elegant neck of an Egyptian princess. She could have claimed a seat in one of the wagons but instead walked along with the rest of the crowd, a black shawl draped over her hair and her expression more interested than saddened.

Longarm lost sight of her in the crowd during the reading of the funeral service. The priest—or preacher, Longarm never did get that sorted out—gave an uninspired sermon that Longarm did not bother listening to. He had heard too many similar talks in the past. Rather, he spent the time looking over the faces among those gathered.

When the service ended and people went their separate ways, Longarm walked back toward the house where neighbors had put Mrs. Oakes in the now empty parlor while helping hands cleared away the plates and pots and platters of food.

Longarm grabbed the chairs that had supported the coffin and carried them back to the kitchen. That earned him a smile of gratitude from the widow.

He took that as an opportunity and pulled an armchair close to Mrs. Oakes.

Maud? No, Molly, he remembered. Molly Oakes. He hitched his chair a little closer and tried to paint a look of concern and helpfulness on his face.

"Ma'am. Could we talk?" he said.

Chapter 20

"This must be a terrible day for you, Mrs. Oakes," Longarm said in a soft voice as he leaned forward on his chair, putting himself close to the widow. "I understand that and I am truly sorry to intrude on you like this."

He pulled out his wallet and laid it open to display the badge, then introduced himself.

"I'm here to help in the meager way that I can. Nothing I can do would ever bring your husband back to you, but at least I may be able to find the person who murdered him and bring that man to justice."

"You are . . . a marshal, you said? A United States marshal?"

"Yes, ma'am. Deputy to U.S. Marshal William Vail in Denver. I'm here representing the Justice Department of the United States. We, all of us, want justice for Mr. Oakes."

"It is because he was guarding the mail, isn't it?" the lady asked.

Longarm nodded. "Yes'm. That's true."

The widow sighed. "Farley was so very proud to have been chosen to protect the mail." She looked at Longarm. "Not everyone can do that, you know."

"Yes, ma'am."

"It was a very great honor."

"Yes'm."

She sighed again and looked off to something he could not see.

"Was your husband happy in his work?" Longarm asked.

"He was at first. Later, toward the end I mean, he began to feel that he was not appreciated. That he should receive more pay for all that responsibility." She wrung her hands in her lap. "Land sakes, Marshal, I don't know where all the money went. Farley made a perfectly adequate salary and we did just fine with it for years. Then recently," she shrugged, "I don't know what could have changed, but it seems we were strapped so much of the time. He got so he talked about money so much of the time." She began to cry. "I don't know why, Marshal. We didn't really need all that much, but Farley worried about it all the time. And those friends of his. He began going out on the nights he didn't work. I never knew his new friends. The ones I saw I didn't like."

"Were they here today?" Longarm asked.

She shook her head. "No, not one of them." She made a sour face and said, "Some friends, huh?"

"Yes, ma'am. Do you know their names, any of them?"

"I never bothered to remember them. Charlie something. And Bo. There was one named Bo. A big man. That one was scary." The lady shivered. "I didn't like him."

"Is there anything . . ." Longarm did not really know how to ask this without causing Mrs. Oakes further distress, but it had to be done. "Is there any chance Mr. Oakes could have, um, cooperated with the thieves who then murdered him?"

Mrs. Oakes drew back in her chair, sitting bolt upright where before she had been leaning toward Longarm. "No!" she declared. "Never."

"Yes, ma'am. Thank you." He smiled. "You've been mighty helpful, ma'am, on this trying day. I'm sorry to've intruded."

"If there is anything . . . Naturally I want you to catch those awful people. If there is anything else you want to ask, I shall be here until tomorrow. The railroad has given me a pass, you understand. I intend to go visit with my sister in Cincinnati. But if you need to ask anything, anything at all . . . I do so want you to catch them."

Mrs. Oakes stood and went back to the kitchen, where neighbors were putting away the last of the foods that had been on the tables outside during the viewing.

Most of those things would spoil before the lady returned from Ohio, Longarm knew. If she ever did return. But at least they would provide her with a basket of eatables to take with her on the train trip east.

Longarm let himself out the front door and went in search of a saloon where he might find a little liquid refreshment himself.

Chapter 21

Longarm had a shot and a beer. The beer was acceptable, but the shot was a corn whiskey and had too obviously been watered. The barman would have been better off to serve some good stuff early in a gent's drinking and the watered product later, after the drinker's judgment had been dulled a bit. It took a really stupid man to start off serving this horse piss. Longarm drank the beer but left half the shot on the bar. He did not even attempt the free lunch. If a man was that cheap with his whiskey, there was no telling what sort of shit he would put out as the free lunch.

He turned to a shabbily dressed fellow standing at the bar and asked, "'Scuse me, but where can I find your town marshal?"

The man set his beer mug down and said, "The station is a block over and, um, three blocks east."

"Thanks." Longarm motioned to the bartender and said, "Give this gentleman another." He laid a quarter onto the bar beside the fellow's mug, tugged his Stetson down, and left. He did not intend to come back to this particular slop chute. There had to be better places in Evanston where a man could find an honest drink.

·

On the boardwalk outside he paused to light a cheroot, then went in search of the police station.

The place proved to be a one-story brick building not far from the Union Pacific roundhouse. There were fly beads hanging over the open doorway. He pushed through them with the soft clatter of wooden beads banging together. A grizzled man sitting behind a raised desk looked up from his dozing and scowled at Longarm, presumably for the intrusion. Perhaps the woman he was daydreaming about was a peach.

"What d'you want, mister?"

"I'm lookin' for the police chief."

"Chief Harney is across the street taking an afternoon break," the desk sergeant said.

"Thanks," Longarm said, smiling and touching the brim of his hat to the man. He turned and went back outside, rattling the beads again on his way out. Once he was clear of the doorway he muttered under his breath, "Asshole!"

There were three businesses directly across the street. A tailor, a general mercantile, and a two-story saloon.

Longarm did not have to ponder long or hard to decide where he should look for Harney. He headed for the Tenpenny Saloon.

Chapter 22

Apart from the gent wearing the apron, there were nine men in the Tenpenny—two at one table, four at another, and three bellied up to the bar. Longarm walked to the bar and laid a silver dollar down.

"Shot and a beer," he said. "Rye if you have it."

The bartender nodded. "We have it." He produced the drinks and returned eighty cents in change. Tenpenny, indeed, Longarm thought. This was even better than a bit house where it was two bits for two drinks or thirteen cents for one. He liked this. Liked it all the better when he tasted the rye whiskey the man served him. It had a fine, crisp flavor, and the beer that went with it was sharp and fresh. Longarm saluted the bartender with his mug and asked, "Where can I find Police Chief Harney?"

The bartender nodded toward the table where four men were playing cards. "The chief is the heavyset gent on the far side of the table."

"Thanks." Longarm left his empty shot glass on the bar, but picked up what was left of the beer and carried it over to the card table.

Chief Harney went past heavyset. The man was hog fat, with belly and jowls to match. He wore a stained dark suit that needed cleaning a couple months back, a shirt with no collar attached, and a dusty black fedora. He needed a shave.

All four men looked up when Longarm approached their table.

Longarm smiled and nodded and said, "Sorry to interrupt, gentlemen, but I need to speak with the chief there. Official business."

Harney did not look pleased to have his game disturbed. He growled, "See my man at the station. Across the street."

Longarm's smile remained fixed. Strained, perhaps, but firmly fixed in place. "It's you I need t'see, Chief."

Harney stood, and it was a damned good thing that looks could not kill. "I already told you where you can go."

Longarm's benign smile was replaced with sheer ice. "My name is Custis Long, Chief. Deputy United States Marshal Custis Long, and I need to speak with you as a matter of official business." He stepped around the table until he was nose to nose with the man and added, "Do you understand me, Chief Harney?"

He set his beer mug down on the card table and gave Harney a cold stare.

Harney dropped his eyes away from Longarm's and took half a step back, stumbling on the chair that was behind his knees but quickly righting himself. He looked down at his companions and said, "I won't be long. Wait for me."

Two of them nodded. One did not bother.

Harney cleared his throat and shot his cuffs. He tried to look tough and in charge when he said, "This way," and led Longarm outside and across to the police station.

Chapter 23

The farther he got from the Tenpenny the more confident and assertive Chief Ronald Harney became. By the time they stepped into the town marshal's office, he was practically swaggering. It was an interesting change, Longarm thought, and he wondered what the cause of it might be.

"All right now . . . what did you say your name is?" Harney demanded once he settled his bulk into a huge chair with cushions piled on the seat. He waved his desk sergeant away with a flick of his wrist.

Longarm gave his name again. Introduced himself all over again and pulled out his wallet and badge to display.

"Yes, yes, no need for all that, I believe you, dammit," Harney said impatiently. "Now, what is this official business that is so damn important you have to disturb a man's card games?"

"One of your citizens has been murdered, that's what," Longarm said.

Harney sat up straighter. Or so Longarm thought. It was a little hard to tell, the way he crouched in the big armchair like a toad on a rock. "One of my people? That is the first I've heard of it. Who? What happened?"

"I'm talking about Farley Oakes, the fella whose funeral was held this afternoon."

"Oh. That," Harney said, again waving a dismissal of the matter. "Not my jurisdiction. Surely you people know about jurisdiction and such as that. Didn't happen here."

"No, it didn't," Longarm agreed, "but the man was one of your citizens. And the mere fact that a crime was done oughta be of concern to any lawman." He paused for a split second, hardly enough to be noticeable, and added, "If he's any good."

Harney's jowls quivered in indignation. He leaned forward a little and stabbed a forefinger in Longarm's direction. "Don't you be coming into my town . . . *my* town, damn you . . . and making accusations, mister."

Longarm gave him a bland "who me?" expression and said, "No accusations, Chief. No, sir, none at all. Just sayin'."

"I don't know why you want to talk to me about Oakes anyway," Harney said. "I barely knew the man. And he wasn't killed anywhere near here. My job ends at the town limits, and that is all there is to it."

Longarm gave the man a cold-eyed smile and spread his hands. "Then I suppose there is nothing you can help me with."

"Of course not. Why could I?" Harney spat back at him.

Longarm's smile quickly faded. "Because your citizen Oakes opened that express car door to someone. Someone who robbed the mail and murdered Oakes. Because Oakes almost certainly had to know whoever it was that killed him. Because this here is where Oakes lived and where it's most likely he became acquainted with his murderer and agreed to cooperate in the robbery. And mostly because it is your job to do whatever you can to solve any crime, anywhere." The cold smile returned. "That's why, Chief."

"I don't think I like you, Mr. . . . what did you say your name is again?"

"You got it the first time," Longarm said. "You're just bein' pissy now." He stood. "Sorry I disturbed your card game, Harney. It's just that I didn't know you would turn out to be so useless." He turned on his heel and headed for the door.

Chapter 24

Longarm walked back to the Elkhorn and upstairs to his room. He pulled off his shirt, dumped a little water from the pitcher into the basin, and gave himself a quick wash using his own soap—he knew better than to count on finding a decent bar of soap in a strange hotel—and the hotel's washcloth and towel. He felt a hell of a lot better when he was done.

He put on a fresh shirt, wadded the worn one into a ball, and tossed it into a corner. Later, he figured, he could send his soiled things out. Lord knew there were enough Chinese laundries in Evanston. Likely he could have his things back fresh and ironed in the morning.

He went back downstairs and asked the clerk on duty, a very young man, thin with a poor excuse for a mustache, where he might get a good meal.

"We have a café attached to the hotel, sir."

"I know. Ate there this mornin'. I'm thinking something . . . no offense, mind . . . I'm thinkin' of something, uh . . ."

The clerk smiled. "I understand, sir. Something a little nicer. There's a very nice place in the next block. Same side of the street. I'm sure you will like it."

Longarm thanked the fellow, went back outside, and turned in the direction indicated.

It was still fairly early, but the place was already beginning to fill up. Longarm recognized several people he had seen at Farley Oakes's funeral, one of them the rather striking woman with auburn hair who had been there and whom Mrs. Oakes so obviously disliked. She was sitting alone at a table intended for four.

She might well have been the woman who had been asking personal questions about the dead express messenger, he thought, the one Chet Powers mentioned to him after the Evanston telegrapher wired an inquiry to Cheyenne about her.

On an impulse Longarm headed for her table and stopped beside it. She gave him a questioning look.

"I'm wondering, miss, if I can set at this table with you. The place is gettin' full an' it seems a shame to use up an entire table for just the one person. If it wouldn't offend you, that is."

"No, no offense at all, Mr. . . . ?" She allowed the question to hang in the air.

"Long, miss. Custis Long."

She held out a small, nicely manicured hand. He lightly touched the offered fingertips, and she said, "I am Beatrice Raven. Bea to my friends. Please sit down, Mr. Long."

"Thank you, Miz Raven. Is it, um, Miss or Mrs. Raven?"

He thought he saw a flicker of smile. "Miss," she said. "Is that important?"

"Oh, I'm sure it's important to you. Not to me, though. I'm just curious. No offense."

"None taken." She tilted her head to the side and peered across the table at him, then said, "Didn't I see you at dear Farley's funeral this afternoon?"

"Aye, you did."

"Did you know him well?"

Longarm shook his head. "No, I didn't. You?"

"Not terribly well, I'm afraid. What did you think of him?" she asked.

Longarm only shrugged. He was saved from further inquiries by the arrival of a waiter carrying her meal of roasted chicken and boiled vegetables.

"What may I bring you, sir?"

"Steak, son. Tallow-fried an' taters on the side. Plenty o' gravy to slop over it. You likely know how cow folk like their steak. Just make sure it spills over the plate on both sides."

"Yes, sir. Very good, sir."

The woman across the table from him was not as young as he'd first thought. She was at least well into her thirties, perhaps in her forties. She had green eyes flecked with gold. Large eyes. And some sort of powder applied around them for emphasis. The dusting of silvery, colored powder worked. He was drawn to her eyes. Could hardly look away from them.

He had noticed earlier in the day how slim she was. And that neck. It was really quite patrician.

She had high cheekbones and lips that were very red. Her lips were full and appeared to be soft. He would not have minded being able to find out about that for himself.

"It is rude to stare, Mr. Long," she said.

Longarm did not look away. This was a woman who surely was accustomed to being stared at.

At the funeral, he'd noticed, she had seemed not to belong. He was sure of that. He wondered what Mrs. Oakes might have to say about her. Perhaps tomorrow he should find out.

The waiter came with his steak, and Miss Raven finished her much lighter meal, dropped a coin onto the table, and excused herself.

Longarm sighed. Damned good-looking woman, he thought. Every head in the restaurant turned to follow her to the door when she left, the men with lust in their eyes and the women with jealousy. Longarm was no different from the other gentlemen. He would have liked to have some of that too. Not that it was apt to happen. But still, a man could yearn without restraint.

Chapter 25

Longarm wandered over to the Tenpenny—Harney and his cronies were at their card table again, but Longarm ignored them—and had a few shots of rye with a beer chaser, then went back to the Elkhorn, calling it an early night. And not a very productive one that he could see. Still, a man does what he can, that being all he can do.

In the morning he woke refreshed after the unusually long sleep and went downstairs for breakfast at the hotel café. He was halfway through his meal when Miss Raven walked in. She paused in the entry to survey the room. When she saw Longarm, she headed straight for his table.

"May I join you?"

"Of course." He quickly stood and went around the table to pull a chair out for her.

"Thank you," she said, stripping off her gloves. This morning she was wearing a very handsome bottle green dress in some fairly heavy material. He guessed she was from a much warmer climate than the chilly mornings of Wyoming Territory. Certainly she was not a local woman or she would not be eating at the hotel. The only females who might do that would be whores, whether amateur or professional, and Beatrice Raven was most assuredly not of that stripe.

The waiter hurried to their table and stood poised to take her order. The man had not been in that much of a hurry when he consented to accept Longarm's order.

"Porridge," she said. "Just a small bowl. With cream, no sugar." Longarm made a sour face. "And coffee, cream only."

"You don't like sweets?" he asked.

"Love them," she said. "They make me fat."

"You're far from that."

"And that is exactly why I do not eat sweets."

"May I ask you something?"

She gave him a very small smile. "You just did, didn't you?"

"I suppose I did at that."

"What is your question, Mr. Long?"

"I got to wonder what you're doin' in Evanston."

"Why, I came for the funeral, of course."

"All right. Perhaps I shoulda asked what you're doin' paying attention to a nobody like Farley Oakes. You didn't know the man when he was alive. Or anyways, if you did, it wasn't here and it wasn't anything his widow would know about him."

"And how would you know such a thing, Mr. Long?"

"It don't take a blind hog to root out an acorn, Miss Raven."

"How quaint," she said.

"What is?"

She laughed. "You, Mr. Long."

Longarm snorted and took a swallow of his morning coffee. "That might could be, Miss Raven, but I'm guessing you never once so much as met Oakes."

"You are quite wrong, Mr. Long. Farley and I became acquainted in Cheyenne. We became friends. When I heard he was killed, I naturally came to pay my respects."

"Bullshit," he said.

The woman's eyebrows shot up. "Mr. *Long!*"

"Oh, don't act like you never heard the word." He paused. "Or is bullshit two words?"

"One, I believe."

"Thank you. Anyways, if you knew Oakes all that well, what color were the man's eyes?"

Bea Raven sucked in a rapid breath, hissing through her teeth. She sat there for a moment nonplussed. Sat there too long actually. "Brown," she said.

Longarm shook his head. "You thought about that too long," he said, "and came up with the most common color. It's a good guess, but Oakes's eyes was blue." The truth was that Longarm had not the faintest idea what color Farley Oakes's eyes had been. His point was that Bea Raven did not know either.

The woman sagged back in her chair and sighed. "All right, dammit, I did not know the man."

"Then what's your interest in him?"

The waiter appeared with her bowl of oatmeal and a cup of black coffee. Raven waited until the man left before she answered. "I . . . I would rather not say."

"All right. Fair enough," Longarm said. "When I'm done here, I'm gonna walk over an' see the widow one more time before she leaves."

"She is leaving?" Raven asked.

Longarm nodded. "Gonna visit with relatives back east someplace. I want to talk to her before then. You might wanna walk along with me. See if she'll answer your questions today."

Raven finished her skimpy breakfast and sat waiting while Longarm finished eating his much more substantial meal. When they were done, Longarm signed a chit for both, putting the meals on his hotel account.

Raven got up and linked her arm with his when they left the café. She repeatedly bumped her hip against his, he noticed. Did it much more than could be accidental too.

He smiled softly to himself as they sashayed along the streets of Evanston, W.T.

Chapter 26

A youngish woman, very pregnant, waddled to the door in response to Longarm's knock. She pushed the screen door open, glared at Beatrice Raven, and gave Longarm a rather skeptical look. She said nothing.

"We'd like to see Miz Oakes," Longarm said, quickly removing his Stetson and holding it in front of him, partially out of simple politeness but also to get his Colt out of sight, pregnant women being often distrustful of firearms and of men who carried them.

"Mrs. Oakes can't see you. She's busy packing."

Longarm nodded and smiled and tried his best to look inoffensive. "Yes'm. She's fixing to go east. I know. That's why I need to speak with her now. Before she gets on that train and I won't be able to talk to her."

"I'm sorry. She is busy and she can't see you. Now, please go." The young dragon hissed once, backed away from the doorway, and closed the front door of the house, leaving Longarm and Miss Raven standing there staring at the screen door.

"That went well, didn't it," Bea Raven said softly.

"Yeah," Longarm agreed in a dry tone. "Splendid."

"We could walk around back and try to catch someone at the well."

Longarm shook his head. "Fat lotta good that would do. Just piss people off." He quickly looked over to his companion. "An' don't go lookin' shocked. You've heard that word before too."

"I wasn't going to say anything. May I make a suggestion?"

"Sure. Whatever you're thinkin', spit it out."

"I'm dying for a drink, and these benighted rustics won't let me inside one of their saloons unless I'm accompanied by a man. Could we go somewhere and get a drink? I'll buy if that is an issue."

"Oh, it's no issue to me." He grinned. "But I'm not one to turn down a free drink, never mind who's paying for it. Come along. I've got kind of fond of the Tenpenny."

They walked together, Bea Raven's hip still making contact with Longarm's much too frequently for it to be accidental.

All eyes swung toward them when they entered the Tenpenny. Longarm knew good and well those looks were not for him. Bea was a hell of a lot better to look at than either of the painted girls who were on offer toward the rear of the place.

Longarm guided Bea to a table adjacent to the one where Ronald Harney and one of his pals were playing gin rummy—a game choice Longarm thought was entirely appropriate. He held a chair for Bea, then seated himself opposite her, where entirely by coincidence he could keep an eye on the fat police chief. There was something about that man that Longarm just plain did not like. Or trust.

The bartender picked up a towel and came over to the table. "What will it be, folks?"

"Do you have a white wine?" Bea asked.

"Lady, this is a saloon. We got four kinds of whiskey and two brands of beer. If you want wine, get on the next train west and go to San Francisco. Or back east. But don't be looking for no lady drinks here in Wyoming."

"Yes, sir." She gave the man a perfectly dazzling smile. "May I please have a shot and a beer."

"Water on the side?" the waiter asked.

"Don't bother."

"Yes, ma'am. You, sir?"

"Rye and a chaser. And keep them coming."

The fellow gave Longarm a grin and a wink and backed away.

Longarm knew good and well what the man was thinking.

And it was not a bad thought, at that. Bea Raven would be enough to get any man's dick hard.

"Here's to you," Longarm said when their drinks arrived. He tossed back his whiskey and Bea handled hers just as efficiently.

Chapter 27

Longarm was not entirely sure how the two of them wound up where they did. Or whose idea it was that they buy a bottle and take it up to Bea's hotel room so they could drink in privacy.

He was not entirely sure how her dress came to be unbuttoned in strategic spots. Or how he ended up sprawled in her bed—damn thing was much bigger and much softer than his even though both were in the same hotel—with his boots off and his vest hanging open. Or how that bottle had gotten so far down toward being empty. Or just exactly why Bea was lying snuggled tight against his side now with her pretty face only inches from his.

"Tell me, sweetie," she said, kissing his ear and lightly running the tip of her tongue around and around it. "Tell me how you know Farley. Tell me everything you know about him. Be good to me, sweetie. Tell me."

Longarm rolled his head to the side so they were eye to eye. He licked suddenly dry lips. Then kissed her. Her mouth was every bit as soft as he had imagined. Tasted good too. Like rye whiskey, although that was probably not an everyday thing. But right now she certainly tasted like rye.

Bea giggled. "You're sweet, Custis. But won't you tell me about dear Farley?"

"I was hopin' you'd tell me," he said.

Bea kissed him. She ran her tongue quickly into his mouth and out again. "Tell me, darling."

Longarm reached inside one of those gaps in her bodice. Her breast was small but firm. Her nipple was tiny and hard as marble.

"In a minute, dear," she said. "First tell me about Farley. Please?"

"Farley robbed the train," Longarm said. "His pals took the mailbags an' killed Farley once they didn't need him no more."

"Yes, of course, but which one of you did that?"

"*Me?*" Longarm exclaimed, jumping bolt upright and snatching his hand away from Bea's tit. "You think I had somethin' to do with Oakes's murder?"

"Why, of course, darling. But don't worry. Your secret is safe with me." Bea gave him a sweet, innocent smile. She yawned and stretched, reminding him ever so much of a cat purring before it lashes out at a wayward mouse. The smile became even sweeter if that were possible. "Tell me, dear, then we can get back to . . . you know." She reached up and touched his cheek. "Come back down here, darling."

Dear, darling, bullshit, he thought. But then he was not half as drunk as Bea seemed to think he was.

"My secret," he repeated. "Just who do you think I am and what do you think I know about ol' Farley?"

"But weren't you working with him, dear? And won't you share a little of that payoff with Mama?"

Longarm shifted to the edge of the bed and stood. He laughed. "You got strange ideas, lady. Wrong ones. I ain't no part of the gang that killed Farley Oakes, and I don't have the least idea who any of them might've been. You are barkin' up the wrong tree." He cocked his head to one side and chuckled. "Though I would purely admire to finish what almost got started on that there bed. You do know how to get a man's blood up. But then you already know that, I reckon."

"You aren't . . . really aren't?"

He reached down for the coat he had discarded on her bedside chair, brought his wallet out, and flipped it open.

"Oh, my God," she croaked. "You are . . ."

"Deputy United States Marshal Custis Long, ma'am. And I was thinking that *you* were part of the gang that murdered Farley Oakes."

Bea began to laugh.

"Lady, surely it ain't all that funny that I'm a deputy, is it?"

"Oh yes. Yes, it is," she said, having to pause twice to catch her breath and wipe her eyes. "Yes, it really is. I'm . . . I'm . . . You see, Custis, I am an investigator for the Treasury Department."

"Treasury? What the hell interest does Treasury have in this murder?"

Bea sat up, wiped her eyes again, and said, "We have no interest in the murder, really. But we have a great deal of interest in the set of engraving plates that were in one of those mail pouches en route to the United States mint in San Francisco."

"We weren't told about any of that," he said.

"No, you wouldn't have been. It was all very . . . embarrassing, don't you see. Those plates would allow a counterfeiter to print utterly perfect hundred-dollar bills. The new plates are required to reflect the signature of the new secretary of the treasury. They are replacements for the outdated plates."

"That'd be quite a haul for a counterfeiter," Longarm muttered.

"Wouldn't it just," Bea agreed.

Longarm looked at her and sighed. "I just think it's a damn shame the two of us figured out who each other is before you had time to ply me with more o' what you had on offer there."

She laughed. "Were you enjoying yourself, Custis?"

"Call me Longarm. And yes, I was having a helluva fine time before you went and ruined it."

"Me? I ruined nothing." She giggled. "You really did have a huge boner pushing out the front of your britches. I'm sorry if you've lost it."

He grinned. "I know where t'find it again."

Bea slid off the bed, stood, and reached for her buttons. But instead of refastening them she began the task of opening them one by one.

It took her less time to shed her dress than it took Longarm to get out of the rest of his clothes.

Chapter 28

Bea's hip bones, hard and sharp and prominent, jabbed into Longarm's belly every time he thrust forward. That was one of the dangers of fucking a skinny woman. Under the circumstances he was willing to put up with it, those circumstances being that he was at the moment deep inside the woman's scrawny body. And there was nothing skinny, scrawny, or less than delightful about her pussy. She was wet and eager and she gave a man a good ride.

She was a busy little wench too. While Longarm was engaged in pumping and thrusting, Bea was every bit as busy herself, pumping her hips upward to meet his thrusts, grunting softly into his ear with the effort and raking his back with her fingernails.

If this little dalliance continued, he thought, he might want to pay for a manicure for the girl. And to get those nails cut down to the quick.

"Ouch," she mumbled after one particularly vigorous thrust. "That hurts."

"Sorry. I'll slow down a little."

"Don't you dare," she squealed. "I'm not complaining. It hurts good."

Longarm began to laugh. This was not a good time for laughter, but he could not help himself. "It hurts good?"

Bea nodded vigorously, her hair tickling his ear when she did so. "It does," she insisted. "It feels . . . It fills me. I can feel it bumping into something inside there. But I like it. Don't you dare stop. If anything I want you to fuck me harder."

"As you wish, ma'am," he said, then pulled back and rammed his dick into her just about as hard as he could manage.

"Ah. Yes. I love it."

"Listen, if you don't quiet down a mite, they are gonna throw us out o' this hotel. Then where will we be?"

"We could go down into the alley and fuck there. I haven't had it in an alley in ever so long," Bea said. The bantering tone of her voice suggested that she was not serious about having done it in an alley before. But Longarm was not entirely sure she was lying. She could well have been telling the truth for all he knew.

What he did know for certain sure was that Beatrice Raven was a mighty good piece of ass.

He felt the rise of his sap and redoubled his efforts until both of them were grunting and pounding, their bellies slapping wetly together with each down thrust.

Longarm came, the glorious rush of it sending him deeper than ever, hurting her, banging the head of his cock into the upper reaches of her pussy. He thrust one final time and stopped, shivering with the intensity of sensation, holding himself rigid above her.

Bea clutched him with arms and legs alike. And with the lips of her pussy, as she too reached a climax. She panted as hard as if she had been running an uphill race. He felt her body ripple and flutter around his cock.

"Whew!" she mumbled into his ear. "That was . . . powerful. I actually came. I don't usually do that. But this time . . . I liked it."

Longarm grinned. "Glad ya did, ma'am."

"Ma'am? So formal?"

He laughed, then rolled off of her so they were lying side by side on the soft bed. He felt cool, almost cold, as the air dried the sweat and cum on his body.

He looked down at Bea's skinny form. Her tits almost disappeared when she was lying on her back. Her ribs were prominent, as were the sharp points of her hips. Her legs were so thin it was a wonder they could hold her up. But there was nothing small about the pleasures she could give a man.

"Would you mind if I have a smoke?" he asked.

"Not at all. Will you mind if I do?"

He raised an eyebrow. Bea laughed, pulled out a drawer in the bedside chest, and reached inside. She brought out a package of ready-rolled cigarettes and a box of matches. She offered him a cigarette, which he accepted. Bea struck a match and held the flame to the tip of his, then lighted her own.

She moved a china saucer from the chest to her soft belly and set it there as an ashtray they both could reach.

The cigarette did not have the strength of flavor of one of his cheroots. It was a drier taste but not a bad one.

The two lay together like that while they smoked in silence. When they were done, Longarm asked, "So tell me, d'you like to suck cock?"

Bea giggled. "It is one of my favorite things, dear. Shall I show you when you are ready again?"

"Oh, I'm ready," he said. "An' yes, I wouldn't mind were you to show me if you're any good at it."

Bea set their ashtray back on the top of the chest, then dipped her pretty head to Longarm's crotch.

Chapter 29

"We seem to be at a dead end," Bea said over a late lunch. She took a tiny sip of the soup that was her entire meal and dabbed at her mouth—very nice mouth, Longarm thought appreciatively—with her napkin.

Longarm shook his head. "We ain't licked yet." He grinned. "Well, maybe I been licked at that. But we're far from bein' at a dead end."

"What next then?"

"I'm assuming that shipment was supposed to be a secret. Tell me what you know about it."

Bea took another small sip of the soup. It was supposed to be a clam chowder, but Longarm had yet to spot any clams. Mostly it looked like milk and butter with some pepper floating on top, but Bea was not complaining so why should he care? She laid her spoon down and thought for a moment, then said, "The plates were shipped by registered mail. That way we knew they would have an armed escort all the way through to San Francisco. We've shipped plates that way before and never had any problems."

"Who knew what was in the package?" Longarm asked, interrupting.

"Our own people, of course. But they are all trustworthy.

A person does not just show up at Treasury and fill out a form in order to work there. The Secret Service investigates every employee very thoroughly. I think we can rule out all of our people."

"All right," he said, "who knew outside Treasury?"

"No one that I know of," Bea said. "There would have been no reason for anyone at the post office to know. To them it was just another package going west."

"But it was addressed to the San Francisco mint, right?"

"Of course," she said. "We had to tell them where it was going, Custis. But not what was in it."

"You reckon somebody could've guessed? Was there a return address, for instance?"

Bea seemed to turn a bit pale, and he thought he might have struck a nerve about the return address, but all she did was shrug and say, "I can't answer that. Anybody *might* have guessed anything they pleased. I certainly couldn't know about that."

"But you don't know of anybody outside of Treasury being aware of what was in that package."

"No. None that I know of."

"Yet somebody obviously did know."

"Yes. Obviously. Otherwise they would have taken more than just the bags consigned to San Francisco," she agreed. She pushed her soup away.

"Damn, woman, can't I get you something to eat more'n that soup? A pork chop or maybe a heap o' mashed taters?"

"No, thank you. Back to the problem at hand, I still think we are at a dead end with this. I'll have to approach the loss from a different direction."

"That's fine if you like," Longarm said. "Me, my worry is more the murder than the theft. I'll look out for the printing plates too, of course. After all, they are federal property and they were stolen from the U.S. mail, but to us the murder of a postal employee is the biggest offense."

"And what will you do about either problem?" Bea asked.

"First," he said with a smile, "I'm gonna finish this lunch . . . You sure I can't get you something more? No? Then I'm gonna look into Farley Oakes a little deeper. He obviously knew the person or persons that killed him, otherwise he wouldn't have unlocked that door. So I'll be looking at him a little harder."

"Mrs. Oakes is already on her way east," Bea said.

Longarm nodded. "True, but she won't be my only source of information."

"*Our* only source," Bea corrected.

"I thought you were gonna look elsewhere."

She shook her head emphatically. "I'm not ready to do that quite yet. Right now I intend to bird dog your tracks."

He grinned. "How close d'you intend t'stay?"

Bea laughed. "Very close." Her eyes dropped toward his crotch, hidden beneath the tablecloth, and she licked her lips provocatively.

"Reckon I can live with that," he said, wadding up his napkin and dropping it onto the table. "Pay the folks, Beatrice. Justice Department don't mind if Treasury stands a treat outa your budget." He pushed back from the table and stood.

Chapter 30

Longarm knocked loudly on the door, waited a moment, and knocked again, louder this time. "Miz Oakes. Miz Oakes, ma'am?"

"Custis, you know good and well there is no one home. I already reminded you, the lady is on a train heading east," Bea said.

He looked down at her and winked. "I know that, darlin'."

"Then why . . . ?"

"For the neighbors if there's any of 'em paying attention. They'll know she ain't home as good as we do."

"All right, but now what?"

"Now," he said, closing the screen door and backing away, "now we break in."

"We . . ."

"Feel free to go back to the hotel if you ain't comfortable breaking a few local laws."

"I'll be right behind you, Custis." Her mouth firmed into a thin line. It was clear she did not like the idea but was determined to go with him.

Longarm stepped down off the porch, glanced at the neighboring houses, and when he saw no one watching, headed around to the back of the Oakes place.

There was a set of clotheslines stretched between T-shaped poles and on the back steps a large wicker basket that would have been for the household laundry. A muslin bag of clothespins dangled from one of the thin lines and one lone dishcloth was pinned beside it.

Longarm mounted the steps to the back porch, Bea following close behind.

"Are you sure . . . ?" she began. By then he already had his pocketknife out and was inserting the blade in the crack between the kitchen door and the jamb.

He winked at her again, gave the knife a tug to flip the latch, and pushed the now unlocked door open.

"That easy?" she asked.

"You've been leading a sheltered life back there in Washington, girl."

"I never said I was from Washington."

"Not originally, I'd say, but it's pretty obvious that's where home is nowadays," he said, holding the door for her to enter first. Then he followed and closed the door behind them.

It was a shotgun house with a narrow front and running deep on a very narrow lot. The parlor, where Oakes had been laid out, was at the front. Then the kitchen. Then a pair of very small bedrooms. The door where Longarm and Bea Raven entered was at the very back, so they found themselves standing in a bedroom, obviously not the one Farley and his wife slept in.

This room held a sagging bed with a pile of clean laundry dumped on it, a chifforobe, and a steamer trunk that was being used as a low table and probably held blankets, or perhaps the lady's wedding dress.

Bea turned to Longarm and whispered, "This place is creepy. It feels . . . empty. You know?"

"Darlin', it *is* empty," Longarm told her. "Ain't nobody home now except us burglars." He grinned. "And why are you whispering, anyway?"

"Am I? Sorry."

"Come on. What we're lookin' for won't be back here."

He led the way forward to the other bedroom, the one where Farley and Mrs. Oakes had slept. It held a double bed, a dressing table, a chest of drawers, and a large armoire crammed into the little room.

Longarm stood for a moment surveying the room, then said, "All right. You go through the dressing table shit and the chest o' drawers. I'll look in the armoire."

"What am I looking for?" Bea asked.

"Anything that might point us toward Farley's friends or tell us where he hung out." Longarm headed for the armoire and began pulling out drawers and going through the pockets of the dead man's clothing.

Chapter 31

"Eureka," he said.

"What?"

"Ain't that what miners say when they've struck gold?"

"I think so, yes, but what did you find?"

"Gold, o' course."

She gave him a skeptical look, and he held up a small, black leather pouch. Longarm turned around—the furniture was jammed in too tightly for him to need, or be able, to take a step—and upended the pouch over the very carefully made up bed. A cascade of gold coins tumbled onto the tulip-pattern bedspread.

"How much . . . ?"

Longarm shook his head. "I haven't counted it, o' course, but there must be two, three hundred dollars there. I'm betting Miz Oakes didn't know about it else she'd have taken it with her."

Bea left the drawers she had been rifling and turned. She pushed the gold double eagles aside one at a time, counting under her breath as she did so. After a minute she looked up and said, "Three hundred. There is three hundred dollars here."

"Like I said, I'm betting Farley was keeping that money a secret."

"It was a bribe," Bea said. There was no room for doubt in either her tone of voice or her disapproving expression.

"Ayuh," Longarm said, "that'd be my guess too."

"That son of a bitch," Bea grumbled. "He got what he deserved."

"Maybe so, but he can't tell us about it now."

Bea scooped up the coins, returned them to their pouch, and dropped the pouch into her voluminous handbag—large and very heavy too, as Longarm could tell by the thump whenever she set it down, leading him to suspect she carried a pistol there.

"Where are you goin' with those?" he asked.

Bea sniffed. "I'm returning them to the Treasury Department where they belong."

"All right but don't let 'em wander off. I might could need those things if any o' this shit comes to a trial. Might need them as evidence."

"If you need them, I can produce them."

"Fair enough then," he said with a nod. "It's all the same government anyhow." He went back to sifting through the things that had once belonged to the late Mr. Oakes.

He heard a footstep in the back bedroom, looked up, and saw a young man holding a double-barreled shotgun that was aimed square on his own belly.

Both hammers, he noticed, were drawn back to full cock. And the young fellow's index finger was inside the trigger guard.

"Hands up," the youngster with the shotgun ordered. "And don't move. We've sent for the marshal. He'll be here soon."

Longarm was not sure, but he thought that damn finger was getting tighter on the front trigger.

Chapter 32

Bea got a stricken look and began to lift her purse.

"For God's sake, Beatrice, don't be reaching in there for your badge. That boy is apt t'think you're going for a gun an' shoot the both of us."

"But I . . ."

"Just hold still, Bea."

"Shut up, you two," the youngster with the shotgun snapped. Behind him three more pushed inside the bedroom, which by now was becoming so crowded there probably would not have been room for another person.

Of the newcomers, one had a small nickel-plated revolver that he held like he was half-afraid of the thing himself. The other two carried short lengths of lumber as if they were cudgels. The whole crowd looked nervous—not a good thing in someone holding a gun on you—and frightened.

"We ain't going nowhere," Longarm said in a voice that he hoped was calming. "You can relax yourselves."

"Just . . . just keep those hands up," the one with the shotgun ordered.

The boy behind him—with one exception Longarm estimated all of them to be in their mid- to late teens—said,

"Throw your gun on the bed. Take it out slow-like and toss it on the bed here where I can reach it."

"All right, but you with the scattergun rest easy. I wouldn't want you t'cut us in half by accident."

"If I shoot your asses . . . Sorry, miss, that kind of slipped out. . . ."

"It's all right," Bea said. "I forgive you."

"Thank you, miss. Anyhow, if I do happen to shoot you, you can be sure it will be on purpose."

"Is that supposed to make us feel better?" Longarm asked. "You said the marshal is coming?"

"Go on now. Toss that pistol on the bed."

Very carefully, using only two fingers, Longarm slid his Colt out of the leather and tossed it. One of the boys with a club leaned forward and snatched it off the covers.

"Come on now," the kid with the shotgun said. "Come out of the house. This way." He motioned with the twin barrels of his shotgun.

Longarm led the way, having to move sideways to get between the bed, which took up most of the space in the little room, and the chest that Bea had been investigating. He came around the foot of the bed and through the narrow space that led to the doorway, Bea following.

Shotgun stepped to the side, and one of the others took Longarm by the arm and pulled him into the back bedroom, shoving him on toward the back porch.

Bea squealed, and out of the corner of his eye Longarm saw that one of them, the big kid, perhaps twenty or a little more, was taking this opportunity of holding power over someone to cop a feel. The burly youngster acted like he was just yanking Bea by the arm and just happened to grab her tit when he did so.

She jerked away from him and slapped him across the jaw, which brought a guffaw from his pals.

"Hold still, bitch. I have to check you for weapons." Then the bastard ran his hands very deliberately over both her tits, bent down, and started to lift her skirts. Bea slapped him again.

Longarm scowled. That boy he would remember. To their credit each of the other boys looked angry also.

"Outside," the one with the shotgun ordered.

Longarm led the way out onto the porch, still holding his hands high, and met another youngster out there, but this one had a badge pinned onto his vest and a large-caliber Remington revolver in his hand.

"Here's the both of them, Tommy," Shotgun said.

"Keep them covered, Whit. You," he said to Longarm, "and, um, you, ma'am. We're going to walk over to the jail, all of us. I'll book you there. Do you understand?"

"Oh, I think we do," Longarm told him. "Can I put my hands down now? My arms are getting kinda tired."

"Right. Hands down, both of you. You, mister, turn around and put your hands behind you so's I can put these cuffs on you. Lady, you . . . I don't know what to do with you. I never arrested a lady before. Just . . . stand there, I guess. Now you, turn around."

Longarm did as he was instructed, and the young deputy, obviously a crony of these boys who had discovered them inside the Oakes house, fumbled a bit with the handcuffs but eventually got them snapped into place.

"All right now. March."

Chapter 33

The desk sergeant gaped when the crowd of junior-grade vigilantes brought Longarm in in handcuffs.

"Good Lord, Tommy. Do you know what .. who ... The chief needs to handle this." The man jumped up from behind his desk and grabbed his hat. "Get those handcuffs off him, Tommy. I'm going to get the marshal."

"Why should I do that, Glenn?" the young deputy asked, but by then the sergeant was on his way out the door, presumably heading across to the Tenpenny where Police Chief Harney hung out.

Despite the instruction from his sergeant, the deputy—or constable or whatever; Longarm was not sure what these people called themselves—did not remove the handcuffs from Longarm's wrists. But he did offer Bea a chair. She sat down and glared at the big youngster who had commandeered the pleasure of massaging her tits.

The bunch of them stood fidgeting and swaying from one foot to the other for three or four minutes. Then Chief Harney waddled into the room, his sergeant trailing unhappily behind. "You," he said, making the lone word sound like an accusation.

"Me," Longarm agreed.

Harney turned his attention to the boys. "What is this all about?" he demanded.

"Whit and these other fellas caught this man and the woman breaking into Miz Oakes's place."

Harney's attention shifted to Longarm. "Is that true, Long?"

Longarm nodded. "We went in there lookin' for clues to who might've held up the mail and murdered Oakes." Without hesitating he added, "We had Mrs. Oakes's permission to make the search." They did not, of course, but the lady was somewhere east along the rails, and no one in this room would be able to ask her about that until, or unless, she came back to Evanston.

"Clues about what?" Harney asked.

Longarm shrugged. "If I already knew that, I wouldn't be needin' the clues."

"And who is this?" Harney asked, looking at Bea.

"She's Beatrice Raven. She was with me," Longarm said quickly. He did not know if Bea wanted her position with the Treasury Department to be known. If she chose to disclose it, that would be fine, but this way Harney could believe anything he liked about why Bea would be with him inside that house.

"Get those handcuffs off the deputy, Tommy," Harney said.

"Deputy?" the kid with the shotgun blurted.

"Yes, you idiot. You have gone and arrested a deputy United States marshal. Now, get them off."

"I'm sorry, sir," the young fellow said while his pal Tommy fumbled to find his handcuff key and get the manacles off Longarm's wrists.

"So did you find anything?" Harney asked while Longarm was being freed.

"Not yet," Longarm told him.

"You are going back there?"

Longarm nodded. "We wasn't done looking when we got, uh, company, y'might say."

Harney cleared his throat and grunted. "Yes, well, I'm sorry about all this."

"No harm done, Chief." He offered his arm to Bea, and the two of them sashayed out of the place. As he passed the big fellow who had made free with Bea's tits, Longarm paused and peered nose to nose with him. Longarm did not speak, but his cold expression said volumes.

"Come on, Custis," Bea implored him, tugging at his arm.

"Right," he said. But he did not move for several seconds. Then he turned, and the two of them walked together back to the Oakes house.

Chapter 34

They were about halfway back to the Oakes house when they heard a loud hail from behind. They stopped, and Longarm turned to see the big youngster with the busy hands coming toward them at a rapid pace.

"What is it you want, asshole?" Longarm asked when the fellow was close.

"I don't like you," the fellow said.

"Good 'cause I don't like you neither," Longarm said.

"You disrespected me back there."

Longarm snorted. "Yeah, it's true enough that I got no respect for you or for any others like you. You are crude and filthy-minded and you don't know how to treat a lady."

"Not that this bitch is a lady. Anyhow I don't care if you are a deputy, mister. You're just some old man to me and I want to beat your ass." He laughed. "Mister, I am gonna hurt you. Hurt you bad."

Longarm's expression changed. From a flinty glare it suddenly became a wide, beaming smile. "Why, sonny boy, I would be purely happy for you t'try that."

"Oh, I would too, except you would probably charge me with something and arrest me." He grinned wickedly. "Or would you be willing to face me and get your ass beat?"

Longarm's response was to beckon the big fellow over to the side of the road and into a vacant lot between two houses. He stopped and removed his hat, his coat, and his gunbelt, handing all three to Bea, who had followed him into the lot.

"Don't worry, Custis," she whispered. "If he beats you too badly, I'll shoot him for you."

He gave her a sharp look, not sure if she was serious about that or not. He decided she was joking. Anyway he hoped she was joking. He turned back to the local fellow. "All right, shit-for-brains. Any time you like."

The boy was big, at least as tall as Longarm and much more heavily built. Very likely he had fought his way to the top of the Evanston heap, beating up smaller opponents, quite possibly rolling drunks in the alleys behind the town's saloons. Longarm was neither appreciably smaller nor addled by liquor. And he had been in a fight or two himself before this.

The local boy balled his fists, lowered his head, and charged straight at Longarm. Longarm stood his ground, then at the last moment seemed to sway very slightly to one side. The local kept charging in a straight line. Until Longarm extended a boot to trip him up and send him tumbling face forward into the weeds.

"Hey!"

Longarm spun and kicked him in the butt, not especially hard but certainly hard enough to get his attention.

The big fellow came to his feet roaring, so enraged that Longarm had to wonder if he had ever found himself in the dirt before.

"You son of a bitch!" He came on again, but not quite so blindly this time.

Longarm's left fist snapped out, bloodying the fellow's mouth and driving a tooth clean through his upper lip.

"Bastard." He threw a punch that likely would have ended the whole thing had it landed as intended, but Longarm's face was not where the punch went. Instead he again swayed slightly to one side and the fist went past his right ear without touching him.

Longarm stepped forward and drove a right hand low to the man's breadbasket. The fellow grunted as the breath was driven out of him. Before he had time to recover from that, Longarm moved forward another shuffling half step and delivered a right, left, right combination to the man's midsection.

The fellow threw a wild swing with his right hand. It missed, and he jerked it into a backhanded swipe that caught Longarm over the right temple.

Longarm again stepped into a combination to the gut and followed that with an uppercut that rattled the man's teeth and sent him rocking back on his heels.

He stepped back another pace, shook his head, and used the back of his hand to wipe some of the blood from his mouth, smearing it across the side of his face in a red mask.

More cautious now, he stalked forward, shoulders hunched and pure hatred in his eyes. His left fist lashed out. Longarm blocked it and answered with a hard left of his own. The fellow tried to duck away, and the punch landed over his right eye, splitting the flesh there and sending another flow of blood into his eye.

That so infuriated him that he once more blindly charged. He ran into the immovable wall of Longarm's right hand. This time he went down, sprawling onto his back. He had yet to land a solid blow on Longarm, while he himself was bloody and covered with dirt and bits of weeds.

"You son of a bitch." It came out as much a moan as an accusation.

The fellow struggled to his knees and glared balefully up at Longarm.

"That's enough, kid," Longarm said calmly. "I don't wanta hurt you." He turned away and reached out to Bea for his things. He had his Stetson on and was about to take his gunbelt from her when Bea's right hand flashed, and a stubby, four-barreled gambler's special, appeared in her hand with a magician's speed.

The little pistol barked, its report light, and a tiny hole appeared in the big fellow's forehead.

He blinked. Then went to his knees and toppled face forward into the dirt, a revolver that had been in his hand falling uselessly with him.

"He was going to shoot you in the back, Custis," she explained and handed Longarm his gunbelt and coat. "He had the pistol in his pocket."

"You're useful t'have around," Longarm said. "Thanks."

"Any time," she said with a smile. "Shall we go get the police chief now and tell him what happened?"

Longarm nodded and strapped the gunbelt around his waist before pulling his coat on. "Yeah," he said. "I reckon we ought to."

"No need now, I think," Bea said, inclining her head toward the street, where some of the big fellow's young friends, including the deputy named Tommy, were approaching at a run.

Chapter 35

It was dark by the time they satisfied Chief Harney's paperwork over the death of the young man, who they learned was Randall Cray. Cray had been an asshole, Longarm thought, but even so his death seemed a shame. A life wasted is always a loss regardless of how it ends.

"Are you all right?" he asked Bea as they walked back out onto the darkened streets of Evanston.

"I'm fine," she assured him. "Killing someone isn't something I do every day, Custis, but I have had to do it more than once in the past. Besides, this was entirely justified and I would do it again. It had to be done, that's all."

Longarm nodded and draped an arm over her shoulders.

"Custis?"

"Mm-hmm?"

"I'm hungry."

He smiled. "Then let's go have us the biggest an' bestest dinner this ol' town has to offer."

"You pick the place," Bea said. "I'll buy."

"By the way," Longarm said, "where'd you hide that popgun o' yours?"

Bea giggled. "Maybe after dinner I'll let you find out for yourself."

"Tell me somethin' like that, lady, and I might insist we skip our supper an' go straight to the search."

She laughed. "Later, dear. I'm starving half to death."

"Then if you insist . . . this way. I saw a place this morning on one o' the side streets. Looked promising, so let's go find out."

Bea walked pressing tight against his side, the warmth of her slim body suggesting a very pleasant evening to come.

Longarm laid his fork aside, belched once, and sighed. "Now that was as good a dinner as I've eaten in," he chuckled, "all day long."

"Oh, quit complaining. It was fine. A little cool perhaps . . ."

"Cool, hell," he said. "Any cooler an' it would've been froze clean through. Damn meat must've come straight outa the icehouse."

"Well mine was just fine," Bea said, carefully folding her napkin and laying it beside her plate.

"It wouldn't have been if you ate real food instead o' that rabbit feed."

She smiled. "You weren't complaining this morning, I noticed."

"Yeah," he agreed, "but you was naked then. A man don't think straight when there's a naked woman close to hand."

Bea laughed until her nose and eyes were running.

"What's so funny 'bout that?" he asked.

"You," she said. "You and the fact that I've never heard a man admit to what all women know anyway."

Longarm chuckled. "The truth is the truth. I ain't denying it. Are you done?"

"Oh, yes. I'm done."

"Good. Now, let's go back to the hotel. You made me a promise a while ago, an' I aim t'hold you to it."

"And what promise might that have been?" Bea asked, her eyes sparkling in the lamplight.

"You know damn good and well what promise. Now, pay these folks so's we can get outa here and, well, you know."

"Oh, I do know, dear, and I intend to keep that promise."

Bea pushed back from the table and he jumped to hold the chair for her to rise.

She paid for their meal—an exorbitant dollar apiece, but at least the amount would go on Treasury's expense books, he thought—and they walked hand in hand out onto the street.

"Longarm. Dear. Would you mind terribly if I . . ."

He never learned what her request might have been. Without warning Bea shoved him in the side, hard, catching him in mid stride and knocking him away.

"What . . . ?"

He heard the dull report of a gunshot at close range behind and the nearly simultaneous thump of a bullet striking something.

Longarm spun, his Colt coming swiftly to hand.

There was a man standing at the mouth of the alley that ran beside the restaurant where they had eaten their dinner. The fellow was holding a Spencer carbine that had smoke curling out of its muzzle. He was frantically cranking the trigger guard to lever a fresh cartridge into the chamber.

Longarm leveled his .45 and fired. Once, twice, a third time.

The man's head snapped back when the first bullet struck him high on the forehead. He tottered forward on suddenly shaky legs as Longarm's second bullet took him in the throat and the third hit his stomach.

His legs collapsed from under him and he fell onto the boards of the sidewalk, the Spencer beneath him. He was dead before he dropped; Longarm knew it.

Longarm turned, in the midst of asking, "Where'd that slug go?"

Then he saw Bea.

And he knew where the ambusher's bullet had gone.

Chapter 36

Longarm dropped to his knees, picked Bea up, and cradled her in his arms.

She smiled at him, blinking rapidly. "It's all right, dear. It doesn't hurt much."

He kissed her forehead and smoothed a wisp of hair back behind her ear. "I'll find a doctor," he said, starting to lay her down on the mud-caked boardwalk.

"No," she protested. "Don't leave me." Flecks of bright blood fluttered on her lips.

"But I have to go get . . ."

"No," she said again, her voice barely a whisper. He had to lean close to hear. "Please. I know . . . I know . . ." She coughed. "I know where I'm shot. I know . . . Custis I could have loved you." She smiled again. "Hell, I do love you. Now tell me that you . . . that you . . . love me."

She was growing weaker. He could feel the life force seeping out of her. "I love you," he said, at this moment not sure if he meant that or not, but he was not going to deny her the request to hear it. "I love you," he said again.

"Custis."

"Yes, darlin'?"

"Custis." She coughed again, and a stream of blood ran out of the corner of her mouth. "Custis, I . . ."

He never learned what the rest of that would have been. Bea went rigid for a moment, then subsided in his arms and was gone.

Longarm laid her down on the boards, then gently closed her eyes. The right eye did not want to stay shut. He had to pull the eyelid down three times before it would stay, and even then he was not sure it would stay put, so he got out a large cent piece and laid the copper onto the eyelid to keep it in place.

He reached down and straightened her skirts. A crowd was gathering by then, and it would not have been seemly for her legs and underthings to be exposed to view.

"Has anyone called the cops?" he asked of no one in particular.

"Yeah," someone said, and a minute or so later a police sergeant came running, revolver in hand. "Clear away. Clear away now."

"You are Long," the sergeant said, even though Longarm was sure he had never met the man.

Longarm nodded. "And you would be . . . ?"

"Dobbs, Henry J."

Longarm stood and extended his hand. "I'm sorry to meet you under these circumstances," he said. "I need to get the lady to an undertaker."

"I can take care of that, Marshal."

"That's kind o' you, Dobbs. Thank you. And do you have a trash collector hereabouts?"

"We do." The sergeant's brow wrinkled. "But why . . . ?"

Longarm hooked a thumb in the direction of the dead man lying in the mouth of the alley. "There's some trash over there as needs to be carted off. Any idea who he was or why he woulda been laying for us?"

"Jesus, there's another one?"

"There is." Longarm nodded. "Bastard got a shot off before either of us could get to him."

Dobbs walked over to the bullet-riddled corpse, turned him over so he could see the face, and said, "This is John Whitmore. Works . . . worked, I mean . . . loading freight, taking coal off the cars, like that."

"For the U.P.?" Longarm asked.

"Yes, sir."

"Is he any kin to the man Miss Raven shot this afternoon?"

"No, none that I know of," Dobbs said.

"Close friend? Anything like that?"

"No, nothing. They didn't even drink in the same places or run in the same crowd."

Longarm shook his head. "Any reason you can think of why Whitmore would want to shoot either of us?"

"No, Marshal. I don't know of anything."

"Any guesses?"

The police sergeant shook his head. "None."

Longarm sighed. "All right then. Tell me where this undertaker o' yours can be found. I'll carry Miss Raven over there."

"I can get an ambulance to do that, Marshal," Dobbs said.

"Thank you, but this is somethin' I need to do myself. For her."

"I understand, Marshal." Dobbs drew himself up a little taller, turned to the crowd, and ordered, "Clear a path there. Let the marshal through."

Longarm bent down, scooped Bea up off the boardwalk, and for the last time cradled her. She felt heavier than she had in life, and her body was already beginning to cool.

"This way, Marshal. Follow me," Dobbs said. "You. And you, Martin. Pick Whitmore up and bring him along, please."

Chapter 37

Longarm saw to Bea's final needs—he had no idea where her things should be sent but assured the undertaker that the Treasury Department would stand good for the costs of her burial—then went over to the U.P. depot to find Doug Baxter, the local night telegrapher.

Baxter was bent over his key sending the evening traffic. He greeted Longarm with a smile, then his expression became grim when he heard the news.

"She was a nice lady," he said. "She stopped in here a couple times to send wires."

"Do you remember the address where she sent those messages?"

"Remember, no. But I would have it on file. Do you need it, Marshal?"

"Not really, but you will. I want you to notify Treasury of her murder, Doug. Will you do that, please?"

"Sure thing, Marshal. It's sad news, though. Any idea why Whitmore shot at you?"

Longarm shook his head. He reached inside his coat and brought out a slim, dark cheroot. He nipped the twist off with his teeth and spat the bit of tobacco into his hand, then struck a sulfur-tipped match aflame and lighted the cigar. "No idea, Doug. Did you know him?"

"John? Of course. He worked in the yard here, you know."

"Who did he hang out with?"

Baxter thought about the question for a moment, then said, "I mostly go home when I'm done here, but John liked to drink and play cards. Mostly he played over at the Tenpenny. I suppose because it is so handy to the depot and the freight yard. You might ask over there."

Longarm's smile was tinged with sadness. "Thanks, Doug. You've been a big help."

"Any time, Marshal. Anything I can do."

Longarm left the U.P. depot and walked over to the Tenpenny Saloon. Chief Harney and his cronies were at their usual table redistributing their pocket money. None of them was apt to become rich that way, but it passed the time and seemed to please them.

"What will it be for you, Marshal?" the bartender asked. He was a man Longarm did not recall seeing before, but he certainly knew who Longarm was.

"Beer, please, an' a shot o' rye."

"Coming right up."

Longarm laid a quarter down and got a nickel in change along with a shot glass of cheap whiskey and a mug of beer with an overlarge head. It was no wonder they were able to make a profit here, he thought. A classier saloon would tip most of the suds off a beer and give full measure in a mug.

Not that he was much interested in drinking tonight. He would be later. When Bea's murder had been properly avenged. Then he might very well cut loose on a good drunk. But not now.

First he wanted to find out why John Whitmore, a man he never heard of, and probably Bea had not either, would come after them.

After *him*!

He remembered Bea shoving him out of the line of fire.

Taking the bullet herself. Not fast enough with her little gun this time.

But that bullet had been meant for him, dammit, not for Bea. Now that he had a moment to reflect on that, he was sure of it.

He tossed down his shot and motioned for another. Took a pull on the cheroot and threw the remaining stub into one of the generous-sized brass cuspidors that lined the floor along the front of the bar.

Son of a bitch! That slug definitely had been his. The more he thought about it, the more certain he was.

A man he'd never seen or heard of had come gunning for him tonight. Spotted him in the restaurant, he supposed. Waited for him in the alley.

And wasn't that mighty damn interesting.

Custis Long just hoped whoever it was that sicced John Whitmore on him would send another. And if that happened, *when* that happened, Longarm intended to see that the cocksucker gave some information this time.

The bartender poured his second rye and Longarm tossed that back too.

"Another, Marshal?"

Longarm nodded.

Chapter 38

Longarm woke up with a splitting headache. He was in his own hotel room. He could tell because the wardrobe was standing open and he could see his carpetbag inside it.

He had no idea how he had gotten back to the hotel. Or, more accurately, who had dumped him here.

No interest in drinking last night, eh? Didn't that turn out to be a load of bullshit. He had gotten rubber-legged drunk.

He blinked and tried to concentrate. On whose damn dime had that occurred? He was fairly sure there was someone—he could hear the voice in his mind but not put a face to it—someone who paid the bartender to keep pouring that rye, which just got to tasting sweeter and sweeter as the level in the bottle went down.

Then the trip up the stairs here in the hotel. At least he assumed it would have been here.

Then . . . nothing.

But why was the wardrobe open? He never left it that way when he quit the room. That was not his habit. There were some things he liked to be tidy about.

Groaning, he stood, made it over to the washbasin, and poured some water in. He splashed a double handful onto his face, then another. Dipped his palm full of water and swished it around in his mouth trying to get rid of some of the vile, morning-after taste that was there. The result was a limited success, but every little bit helped.

Huffing and blowing, he crossed the room—he was barefoot, he noticed now, had no idea where his boots were—ah, there, set neatly at the foot of the bed—to the wardrobe.

He dragged his carpetbag out, set it on the bed, and sat down beside it. Stopped for a moment to shake his head in a useless effort to clear it. Maybe a little hair of the dog would help, but that had to wait. First the carpetbag.

He pulled it open and took a look inside. Everything seemed to be there. Not, however, arranged as he remembered it. His balbriggans were rumpled. He had left them smooth and tidy from the laundry—which reminded him, he needed to collect the things he had sent out to the Chinese laundry here in Evanston—and his spare collar was folded so close together that it had a crease in the celluloid. "Shit!" he mumbled under his breath. That would never come out. Now he would have to buy a new one.

Someone had rifled through his things. Nothing seemed to have been taken, at least nothing that he could think of at the moment. But someone most definitely had gone through his bag.

The same person or persons who brought him upstairs last night?

With any kind of luck the desk man downstairs could tell him who that had been.

Even if he learned that, though, the bigger question would remain: Why?

Almost certainly it would have to do with Farley Oakes's murder and the theft of Treasury's printing plates.

He wished Bea were still here. He was fairly sure he would know the plates if he came across them. But maybe not. He was not exactly familiar with the latest goings-on in the printing of money.

Longarm groaned. His tongue felt like it was made of cotton. Dirty cotton at that.

He found his coat carefully hung in the wardrobe. Checked the pockets. Everything was there, everything where it was supposed to be.

Yet he had the impression that his pockets had been gone through, just like the carpetbag had been.

Longarm pulled the coat on, buttoned his vest, and while he was at it, pulled the Colt out of its leather and checked the loads. All cylinders were loaded, the cartridges showing undamaged caps and lead. He tucked the derringer into his left side vest pocket and draped the gold chain across to his pocket watch in the right side pocket.

Then he stood and wobbled down the stairs. First he wanted that hair of the dog, dammit. Then he could start asking some questions.

Chapter 39

Longarm had a beer—just one—no shot this time. Damn rye like to put him under last night. If an assassin had been laying for him then . . . he shuddered to think what might have happened.

"Are you all right, Marshal?" the barman asked when he served the beer and collected Longarm's dime.

"Yeah." He grinned. "More or less. D'you know who carted me outa here?"

"That was Doug Baxter. He heard you singing, came in to see what the caterwauling was. He saw you and dragged you out."

"I'm gonna have to go thank the man," Longarm said. It occurred to him that Baxter might well have done more than merely put him to bed. He might have saved Longarm's life as well. Anyone laying for Longarm might have been shy about stepping out and murdering a deputy marshal when there was a witness. And it was entirely possible that such an assassin could have been a friend of Baxter's and not wanted to kill the man.

One thing, though. Longarm felt fairly sure that Doug Baxter would not have had either reason or desire to rifle through his belongings. That had been done by someone else, probably while he was out making an ass of himself.

Longarm had no evidence of that fact. But he felt it rather strongly. Still, he would try to remember to ask Baxter about it.

He thanked the bartender, whose name he could not remember this morning even though they might have been chummy the night before, and walked down the street to a barbershop.

Longarm was the third person in line. He settled down to wait with a cheroot and a copy of the latest Omaha and Cheyenne newspapers—one of the perks of being in a town on the U.P. mainline. When his turn came, he laid the newspapers aside and hung up his coat but decided to leave his .45 where it was.

After all, someone had sent John Whitmore out to kill him. Whitmore was dead, but that did not necessarily mean the urge had been satisfied. It was very likely that the person would try again, and if an attempt on his life was made, he did not intend for his revolver to be ten feet away hanging on a barber's hat rack.

"So how are you today?" the barber asked, chatting up his customer.

"Poorly," Longarm said.

"Sorry to hear that, mister." Obviously the gent did not know who or what Longarm was.

"Say, you might could help me with something," Longarm said.

"Certainly, if I can."

"There was a fella. Got himself shot last night. I happened to be on the street. Everybody was fussing over some girl that he shot. Me, I bent down to see if I could do for him. He whispered a message to me, but he died before he could finish tellin' me who I was supposed to give it to. I was thinkin', maybe you knew him an' who he ran with. Who he might want t'hear his dyin' words."

"Oh, I knew him," the barber said, working his brush across Longarm's cheeks and leaving freshly whipped lather behind. "In this chair I get to meet pretty much everyone in Evanston. It isn't all that big a town, you know. The man who was shot was John Whitmore."

"So d'you know who the man ran with? Who I maybe should look up for him? I'd hate for a man's last words to not be heard by his friends."

The barber pushed Longarm's head back, brought his razor blade to Longarm's throat, and carefully scraped away the stubble. "I think I might know where you should look," he said.

"It would be the Christian thing t'do," Longarm said.

The barber wiped excess lather onto his towel and bent to the shaving again. Longarm almost thought he had forgotten the question, but in his own good time the man said, "Go see Robby Brandon. He was closest to John."

"Any idea where I might could find Brandon?"

Again the barber took his time. He stropped his razor afresh and finished Longarm's shave before he spoke again. "Mama Chen's."

"This Brandon fella should be there?"

The barber nodded. Tossed his towel into a laundry bin and motioned for his next customer. He seemed almost to have forgotten that Longarm was there.

Mama Chen's. Whoever—or wherever—that was. Longarm dropped a fifty-cent piece on a small table behind the reoccupied chair, collected his coat and hat, and headed out into a cold morning rain.

Chapter 40

"Of course I know Mama Chen. Everybody in Evanston knows Mama. We got so many Chinese here, you know," the man behind the counter at the café said.

"This Mama Chen person is Chinese then."

"That's right." The cook slid a plate of ham and fried potatoes across the counter and collected his quarter. He dropped the coin into a pocket on his apron and added, "She runs an opium den over toward the edge of town. Pretty much all the Chinese go there and a good many white folks too. The thing with Mama is that she's trustworthy. A man can go there . . . or so I'm told, mind you I never been there myself . . . a man can go there and have his drugged-up dreams and know no one will bother him or his pockets while he's there. We got a couple other opium houses in town that you can't say as much for. Things might disappear out of a man's pockets in those. Mama wouldn't put up with anything like that. Fella gets to stealing from Mama or her people, next thing you know his throat would be cut and no one would know who did it."

"What does the town marshal think of that?" Longarm asked, picking up his knife and fork and attacking his breakfast while they talked.

"We pret' much leave the Chinese alone. Any trouble they cause is strictly amongst themselves. They don't bother us whites, and we leave them be in return." He picked up his apron and wiped his hands on it. "That may not be the law, but that's the way it is."

Longarm's only comment was a soft grunt. Like the man said, that was just the way it was here. But it was *not* the law.

The ham was good and salty, probably out of Nebraska, and the potatoes were fried crisp, just the way he liked them. He did not care for a soggy slice of potato. The coffee was good too. Lordy, after last night he needed coffee. His head felt like some son of a bitch had gotten in there and was trying to hammer his way out.

The potatoes helped scrape some of the fur off his tongue though, and the coffee took care of the rest of it.

A man his age really should know better than to let himself go on a toot like that. Especially a man who might have somebody laying for him.

It occurred to Longarm that a man very well might get away with murder in this town. All he would have to do would be to sneak up behind, knock a fellow out, and slit his throat. Harney would assume the killing had been done by one of the Chinese and pay no attention to it.

Or maybe that deliberate ignorance only applied to Chinese that were murdered. It could be that killing a white man here would bring a world of hurt down on the local Chinese. Longarm asked the cook, who was busy making an omelet for another customer.

"No, sir. The Chinese wouldn't think of messing with one of us. They just wouldn't. Except for, well, like I told you."

And how would Harney know the difference? Fact was, he wouldn't. Anything done like it had been the Chinese doing it, the town marshal was very likely to ignore. Of course Longarm was not sure how much Police Chief Ronald Harney bothered with the letter of the law anyway. The man spent all his time in the Tenpenny playing cards with his pals.

Longarm grunted again, then said, "Thanks."

He went back to the task of making his breakfast disappear.

Chapter 41

Mama Chen's was a surprisingly ordinary place. The front looked like any large mercantile you might find in any town. It had a false front and a low roof. But no porch at the front, Longarm noticed. Probably they did not want the customers nodding off in public.

Inside there was a small reception area with an older Chinese woman running the show—obviously Mama Chen herself—and a pair of young, rather attractive Chinese girls sitting nearby. All three wore flaming red dresses, slit up the sides of the lower portions, with bright gold dragons entwined in the pattern. Mama had very short hair, the attendants very long and shiny.

"Good morning, Marshal Long," Mama said when he entered. She dipped her head in a small bow.

"Ma'am," Longarm said, sweeping off his Stetson and bowing in return.

He wondered how the hell she knew who he was. He was sure he had never seen her, nor was it likely that she had seen him. It seemed the old girl kept her eye on everything that went on in Evanston. And everybody.

"How may I help you?" Her English was good. Some Chinese, he knew, pretended to have little English even though they could speak it perfectly well—they apparently believed it was expected of them—but there was no pidgin talk from Mama.

"I'm lookin' for a man name of Robby Brandon. I'm told he comes here."

The woman slowly nodded. She made the simple gesture seem elegant. "Mr. Brandon is one of my favored customers."

"Is he here now?" Longarm asked.

"Regrettably, Marshal, he is not."

Longarm wondered if he could believe her. The man was a regular customer and Longarm was a stranger. Still, he was a stranger with a badge. He probably could not make any real trouble for her—but Mama Chen might not know that.

"Mr. Brandon works for the railroad, you know."

He in fact had not known that.

"At this moment he is elsewhere."

A heavy, sweetish scent drifted through the fly beads hanging over a door in the back wall. Opium. The patrons lay on benches, smoking and nodding off, enjoying the dreams of the pipe. It was said a man could become addicted to the stuff, but it was perfectly legal.

"Do you know when you might expect him?"

"I do not know this, Marshal. Is there anything else I can do for you? A pipe? Perhaps one of these pretty girls?" She gestured toward the pair of attendants.

They were pretty enough. Slender, not very tall, both of them with very long, sleek, shiny hair. One of them feigned shyness and fluttered her eyelashes, which were so long they had to be false.

"Another time," Longarm said. "I'm workin' right now. On duty. But thanks for the offer."

"It would be my pleasure to serve you. Without charge, of course."

So officers of the law got free services here, Longarm thought. He wondered if Harney availed himself of that offer. Longarm had no reason to think that the man did . . . but all the same he thought that the man did.

"Thank you, Miz Chen."

"It is Mama. Please." She smiled. "All my friends call me Mama. You must do so also."

"Yes, ma'am. Uh, Mama. Thanks." Longarm bowed again and left.

Brandon was working, Mama had said. For the U.P. That was reasonable enough. This was a Union Pacific town.

He headed back to the U.P. depot. Baxter would not be on duty now—he had to remember to thank Doug for saving his butt last night—but surely anyone could direct him to Robby Brandon.

Chapter 42

"What time is it?" The on-duty clerk looked at the big Regulator clock on the wall and squinted. "Right now Robby should be about to pull into Ogden. Him and the rest of that crew will turn around there and be back here about, oh, five-fifteen or thereabouts."

"What does Brandon do, exactly?" Longarm asked.

"Brakeman."

Longarm whistled. Being a railroad brakeman was one of the most hazardous jobs there was. Anywhere. Jumping from car to car in rain or sleet or snow, with ice coating the cars, bumpy track, errant tree limbs. The hazards were endless. Longarm had even heard of one poor son of a bitch who was attacked by an eagle while he was walking one of the runways on top of a freight car. The bird knocked him down between the cars and the wheels made bloody mincemeat of him. More brakemen died on the job than men doing any other occupation. Or so *Harper's Weekly* had assured him.

The much safer air brakes—it always amazed Longarm to think that something as insubstantial as mere air could stop an entire railroad train—had been around for years, but a great deal of the nation's rolling stock still depended on mechanical brakes and the brakemen who applied them.

Robby Brandon was part of a dying breed. In more ways than one. In a few more years there would be no such thing as a brakeman who physically moved from car to car, tightening the brake wheels as he went. It would all be done with the Westinghouse system of air brakes. And a good thing too, eliminating all those deaths. Hardly a month went by even now without a brakeman somewhere being in the news.

"About half past five, you say?"

The clerk nodded. "Along about then."

"I'll look for him then, thanks."

It was no wonder, Longarm thought, that Brandon liked to hide in the opium-induced dreams at Mama Chen's. Every day might very well be the last he would ever see.

Longarm's job was dangerous enough. He did not know how he would have reacted to knowing his life expectancy could be measured in months and not years.

While he waited for Brandon to return to Evanston, he thought, he could go back to the hotel for a change of clothing, then over to the undertaker's to make sure Beatrice was being properly taken care of. He wanted only the best for the sprightly girl who had saved his life.

Son of a bitch! He wished John Whitmore was still alive, so he could kill the bastard himself.

And he sure as hell wanted whoever it was that sicced Whitmore on him.

Chapter 43

Longarm had the bellhop bring up a copper tub and some buckets of hot water.

"Would you like me to help you pour, sir?" the young man asked. There was something in his voice that suggested he was more interested in looking at Longarm naked than in helping with the water, so Longarm gently declined. He had no animosity toward queers, but he had no particular love for them either.

"Just pour that first bucket in an' leave the others beside the tub where I can get to 'em."

"Yes, sir." The kid looked disappointed.

Longarm saw him out, then closed the door behind him. He was about halfway through his bath when he heard a light tapping on the door. With a sigh of resignation, Longarm got out, dripping on the rug, and wrapped the much too thin and too small hotel towel around himself.

It would be the bellboy, still trying to get a look at his pecker, he guessed. Well, as small as the towel was, it was very apt to be on display despite Longarm's best efforts to cover up.

"I'm comin'." He stepped over to the door and pulled it open.

Instead of the bellboy a tiny Chinese girl stood there in the bright red dress that seemed to be Mama Chen's livery. She gave him a wide, insincere smile. Then her gaze drifted south to the parts the skimpy towel did not cover and her expression changed. Her eyes became wide and the smile became genuine. She quickly hid behind the flat of her hand and giggled.

Longarm realized what the problem was. He rearranged the towel as best he could and shrugged an apology. "I, uh, I was takin' a bath and . . ."

"I help," the girl said.

"Come again?"

"I help you bath. Wash you dick."

"Wash it? Oh, I couldn't do that. I . . ."

"Yes, please. I help." She pushed her way past him and closed the hotel room door. "Come, please," she said, leading the way to the bathtub.

Longarm shrugged again, this time with resignation, and followed her.

The girl reached down and pulled the towel away from his waist. She giggled a little more and helped him back into the tub.

With rather expert care she took the dish of soft soap and lathered him all over, paying particular attention to his cock and his balls. Longarm leaned back against the slope of the slipper tub and smoked a cheroot while the girl worked him over. He had to admit that it felt pretty damn nice.

"You wait," she said. She removed the cheroot from between his lips and set the slim cigar aside. Then she picked up one of the buckets of water, more warm than hot by now, and sluiced it over him. That got most of the suds off.

She took his hand and tugged, urging Longarm to stand in the now soapy and rather grimy water so she could sponge off the last of the soap and get him squeaky clean.

Her hands lingered on his pecker rather more than was

really necessary. The girl seemed to be contemplating something.

He soon found out what.

She helped him out of the tub, dried him off, and led him to the bed. She pressed him down onto his back and bent over him.

The pretty Chinese girl—she was getting better looking the longer she was in the room, he noticed—licked his cock from root to tip, then in a single motion stripped off her dress.

She was smaller without her clothes. She barely had any tits and had no pussy hair at all. A perfect China doll, Longarm thought.

Giggling, she straddled his legs and bent down to do some serious sucking. Within seconds, less than seconds perhaps, he was rock hard and standing tall. She touched him with rapt wonder, then again sucked him.

She brought him close to the edge, then moved up on his body, still astride him, and lifted herself high enough that she could guide him into her pussy.

Longarm closed his eyes and let the girl do the fucking.

She was good at it. Small and tight and vigorous in her movements. He had been close to coming in her mouth. Now he could hold back no longer. With a sudden, upward thrust of his hips, he drove himself so deep inside her that he could feel the head of his cock bump up against something inside the girl's body. He came with a gush, spurting his fluids deep into her.

"Oh, wow. That was good, honey."

Without a word the girl moved off of him and stepped away from the bed. She got a washcloth, soaped it, and returned to wash his prick, then rinsed the soap out and came back to finish cleaning him.

She brought a towel and very gently dried his cock and balls.

"Nice," he said.

The girl retrieved her dress and let it slide over her head and down her tiny body. Then she bowed and said, "Mama Chen, she say Misser Bran-don friend is there. Waiting for Bran-don, yes? You come if you like."

"I just did come, thank you. And I did like."

The Chinese girl looked confused.

"It's all right, honey. I confuse myself sometimes." He reached out, intending to bring her back to the bed, but she bowed and quickly scuttled out of the hotel room, pulling the door closed behind her.

Longarm smiled. That wasn't a bad way to receive a message.

Chapter 44

The interior of the opium den was dim and smoky. That sickly sweet odor permeated the heavy, motionless air. A very few, low-trimmed lamps did their best to penetrate the smoke and the cloying scent, but their best was not very good at all.

Longarm bent low to get beneath the heavy beams that supported a low ceiling.

Mama said Thomas Budd was on the top bunk, third tier on the left. Longarm moved forward cautiously, crouching, lest he might stumble over something. Not that there seemed to be much in the way of stealth to worry about. The men—and occasional woman as well—who lay on these hard, wooden bunks seemed oblivious to anything outside their own smoky dreams.

After looking at some of these somnolent figures Longarm realized why it was that Mama Chen did not supply regular mattresses or bedding for her customers even though he suspected she would be well able to afford such comforts. As the smokers nodded off, they tended to drop their pipes. Obviously it was of little interest to the proprietors if the customers burned their own clothing, but this way there was less chance that the structure itself could catch fire. Sensible, Longarm thought.

He found the slab where Robby Brandon's pal Thomas Budd was stretched out on his back, sucking on a long-stem pipe and smiling at whatever he saw on the ceiling.

The man was older than Longarm might have expected. He was skinny, probably somewhere in his fifties. He was balding, fringes of graying hair remaining on both sides of his head and, perhaps to compensate, a huge handlebar mustache drooping down from the sides of his mouth.

He looked sleepily at Longarm when the tall deputy approached his pallet. He smiled and nodded as if they were longtime chums.

"H'lo."

Longarm smiled back at him. "Hello, Tom."

"What you . . . doin' here?"

"I came to see you, Tom. And your friend Robby."

"Robby's not here. I started," he paused to giggle a little, "started without him."

"I see that you did, Tom. Would you mind if I ask you some questions?"

Budd waved his pipe airily. "Ask . . . anything. I got no secrets." Then he giggled again. "Well, some secrets. Me and Robby an' the others."

"Yeah, well, you remember me. I'm Robby's pal Custis. You remember, don't you?"

Budd's brow knitted in deep concentration for several long moments, then he brightened and said, his voice giving away the lie, "I remember." He took another drag on his pipe, held the smoke in his lungs for a bit, and finally exhaled.

Longarm thought that if he stayed in here much longer, he would be under the influence of the opium too. "I want you to come with me, Tom. Just outside."

"Can I bring my pipe?"

"Sure thing, Tom. Bring it. I tell you what, I'll even buy you another ball of tar."

Budd's smile was as sweet as that of a small child. "Really? You would do that for me?"

"Sure, Tom. Sure I will."

Budd frowned in concentration again. Then he admitted, "I've forgot your name."

Longarm smiled and took his arm, urging him off the bunk. "It isn't important. Come with me, Tom. We'll go out where we can talk."

Mama Chen had an office off to the side of her reception area. Longarm took Budd there and sat him onto a chair upholstered in bright red velvet. The office was small but opulently furnished in red and gold. Mama Chen quite obviously favored those colors.

Budd frowned. "Why're we here?"

"I want to talk to you about Robby," Longarm told him after he closed the door so Mama and her ladies could not hear.

"What 'bout?"

"I'm worried about him, Tom. This thing he's been involved in, him and John Whitmore. He could get in trouble."

Budd waved that notion away. He chuckled and said, "Can't get in no trouble. Not Robby."

"John did, though."

"Ah, that was diff'ren. Boss won't let that happen to Robby." He belched. "Or me."

"You're involved in it too, Tom? I didn't know that."

"Sure. Me. Robby. The fellas." He shook his head, smiled, took another pull at the pipe in his hand. He was holding the pipe with his fingers wrapped around the bowl, which had to be hot enough to blister the skin, but he did not seem to notice.

"Who are the fellas, Tom?"

"Ah . . . you know."

"What about the boss?"

Budd did not answer.

"I'm worried that Robby and you and the fellas will get in trouble, Tom. I'm worried about you."

Budd scowled and leaned forward. He carefully studied Longarm, his face only inches from Longarm's. Then he snorted and sat back in his chair. "I don't know you."

"I'm Robby's friend Custis."

"Don' know you," Budd insisted, sucking on the pipe again. His eyelids drooped low. Longarm suspected he had gotten just about everything he could out of Thomas Budd.

Longarm left him there and went out to the counter, where Mama and her girls were waiting for more customers. "You can put him back in with the rest of them if you like, Mama. And give him a ball of the tar on me." He took out a dollar coin and laid it on the counter. "Thank you for your help, Mama. If you ever need me to return the favor, you know where to find me."

The little Chinese woman smiled and bowed. And plucked the dollar off her counter. "Thank you so much, mister marshal. I will remember."

"An' so will I, Mama." He thought for a moment, then said, "When Brandon gets in this evening, I want to talk with him. Better be before he starts smoking, I think. Stash him in your office or somethin', then send one of the girls for me, please." He grinned and added, "Just not the one you sent a little while ago." He did not see that girl among the others at the moment.

Mama looked distressed. "That girl. She no good?"

Longarm laughed and said, "Just the opposite, Mama. She was very good. So good if she comes to get me I might not be able to get here in a hurry, and it's important for me to see Brandon before he starts smoking. But no, that girl was very good, Mama." Longarm rolled his eyes and laughed again.

"All right then. When Brandon, he come, I will send." Her laughter was light as a bamboo wind chime. "Send one ugly girl, yes?"

Longarm was chuckling as he left the opium house and headed for the Tenpenny.

Chapter 45

Longarm was hunched over a beer—the shot that went with it long since consumed—when a Chinese girl in the red and gold silk dress that was the uniform for Mama's girls peeped shyly through the batwings. She caught Longarm's eye and beckoned him. The motion she used was not the crooked finger that an American girl would employ. Instead she held her palm down and swept it toward herself. It was an unusual gesture, but he got the message anyway.

"Yes, what is it?" he asked.

The girl shrugged her shoulders and uttered, "No Englaise, please." She might have been telling the truth. Or not. The few words she did say came out easily enough. She motioned for him to follow, again using that odd, palm down gesture, and led off toward the opium house.

Robby was waiting for him, obviously expecting almost anyone other than the tall deputy. The Evanston railroader was wearing the striped overalls of a train crewman, still soot-smeared from his work shift. He had dark hair, dark eyes. He was in need of a shave. When he saw Longarm come through the door he blanched and gave Mama a harried look as if he were a rat that suddenly found itself cornered.

"He here," Mama said, quite unnecessarily.

"What the hell?" Brandon croaked.

"You an' me are gonna talk," Longarm said. His smile was anything but friendly. "That is, you will talk and I will listen. Right?"

"I, uh . . ."

"Come with me, Brandon. We're goin' over to the marshal's office so's I can borrow me a jail cell."

"Jail!" Brandon bleated. "I haven't done nothing to go to jail over."

"We'll see 'bout that," Longarm said. "You might could be charged as an accessory to the murder of Treasury Agent Beatrice Raven and the attempted murder of another federal peace officer." Longarm's smile was grim and anything but friendly. "Then . . . let's see. There's the murder of a postal employee. And robbery of the mails. That's a federal offense too. Oh, you got you quite a list building up there, Robby."

"What the hell . . . ? I never . . . I . . ." The man blustered and blathered unhappily. Longarm paid no attention to any of it.

"Or it could be that I'll just hold you as a material witness to them same crimes," Longarm said. "What you go in for, and how long, depends on how well you and me get along, how much of what you know you decide to tell me. You understand? You tell it all . . . or I use the big stick against you and charge you with all them crimes. I can do that, y'know, you bein' an accessory. I can charge you just like you pulled them triggers."

Robby Brandon was beginning to look like a very unhappy fellow.

"Now, just to make sure you know how thin the ice is that you're skatin' on, turn around." Longarm said.

"What?"

Longarm's voice hardened. "I said turn around. Now, do it."

Brandon turned.

"Hands behind the back," Longarm ordered.

"Can't you just . . . you know . . . in front."

"No. Now put 'em back here."

Brandon reluctantly complied. Longarm pulled out his handcuffs and snapped them around Robby Brandon's wrists. Then he nodded toward Mama and tipped his hat by way of a thank-you before he led his detainee out of the opium house and back into town.

Police Chief Ronald Harney's desk sergeant looked surprised when Longarm came in.

"What can we do for you, Marshal?"

"I need to park this man in one o' your cells." He grimaced. "I suppose the chief is over to the Tenpenny. Him and his pals were at their usual table when I left there a little while ago."

"I wouldn't know anything about that, Marshal," the sergeant said.

"No, I'm sure you wouldn't. Go get him anyhow. Tell him he's cooperating in a federal investigation. Me, I'm gonna lock this man up till he tells me what I need to know."

"Yes, sir, Marshal." The desk man, a short, stocky fellow with chin whiskers that bobbed and bounced when he spoke, scurried out from behind his desk and out the front door.

Longarm escorted Brandon to a cell and locked him in, then had him back up to the bars so he could unlock his handcuffs and return them to his coat pocket where they belonged.

Brandon looked thoroughly cowed. Longarm figured to let him spend the night as a guest in the fat police chief's jail, then by morning the man should be willing to open up and tell Longarm everything he knew—if there was anything— about just why it was that a complete stranger came gunning for him. "I'll be back first thing in the morning, Brandon."

The prisoner said nothing, just sat with his back to the cell door, his shoulders set in sullen defiance.

"First thing," Longarm repeated.

He went back to the front of the police headquarters and

waited for the sergeant to return. When he did, the man said, "The chief will be over directly."

"That's fine," Longarm said. "I'm going on to supper. Just you make sure he knows that man in there is being held for federal charges. No bail. You understand?"

"Sure. No bail, no release, no nothing. Robby is your prisoner, not ours."

"Exactly," Longarm said. "And I thank you." He tipped his Stetson in the man's direction, then turned and headed for the café where he and Bea had so recently had that last meal.

Chapter 46

Longarm's meal was not a happy one. Bea Raven should have been across the table from him. Instead he was dining alone and did not like it. His meal came with a salad, which he ignored, and a huge, perfectly prepared steak, which he ate only part of, his appetite gone almost before he sat down at the table.

He had *liked* that girl, dammit. Now . . .

He stood, ignoring the offer of a dessert or more coffee, and tossed both his napkin and a half dollar onto the table. Longarm was just on his way out the door when he heard the dull report of a distant gunshot followed closely by another. That was nothing to get excited about, of course. Drunks and other idiots were constantly firing their pistols into the air—although God knew why they would do such a stupid thing.

The gunshots reminded Longarm that he really ought to go back to the hotel and clean and oil his .45, it being only sensible for a workman to take care of his tools.

Better yet, he thought, he would stop by the jail. They should have a cleaning rod, cloth patches, and some whale oil there that he might borrow to complete the job.

With that in mind he altered direction and increased his

pace. He paused once to strike a match and light a cheroot—
he was running low on those and reminded himself to stop
at the mercantile first thing in the morning and buy some
more—before continuing on.

When he got to the jail, the desk sergeant was not behind
the desk where he usually sat. The door leading back to the
cells stood open, so Longarm went to it, intending to check
on his prisoner. Inside he found the cell door standing open
and both the sergeant and Police Chief Ronald Harney bent
over Brandon, who was lying on the floor, arms outstretched,
amid a pool of still spreading blood, permeating the air with
its copper stink.

Chapter 47

Brandon was still alive. Barely. His eyes stared wildly back and forth. Longarm joined the locals and bent over the obviously dying man. Brandon saw Longarm and fixed his stare on the deputy. His right hand flexed and reached, rising off the floor to clutch at Longarm's sleeve.

"Huh . . . huh . . . chee . . . huh." The sounds, more grunts than words, were all he could manage.

Longarm touched the sergeant on the elbow. "Go get a doctor for him."

"Mister, the man is on his way out. You know that. He's shot clean through. What he needs is a burying not a doc."

Longarm's expression hardened. "He is still my prisoner, and I want him to have the benefit of a doctor. So do it. Now!"

The sergeant glanced at his boss, then shrugged. "All right. If that's what you want."

"I do," Longarm snapped.

The sergeant stood and left. Slowly. Ronald Harney gave Longarm a hard look. Miffed because an outsider was ordering his people around? That could be, Longarm thought. If it was . . . tough shit. If there was any chance at all of saving Robby Brandon's life, he wanted to try. For two reasons, first being that Brandon was in Longarm's custody and he was responsible for him, and second being that Brandon had information that Longarm damn well wanted. If he died, that knowledge died with him. Longarm did not want that to happen either.

"Huh . . . huh . . . ," Brandon croaked.

"Just lie still," Longarm told him. "We got help on the way."

The words seemed to give no comfort to Brandon. After a few moments his heels drummed on the stone floor of the jail cell. His eyes went wide as he stared into a world Longarm could not imagine, and then he was gone, mouth gaping open and empty gaze fixed on Longarm.

Robby Brandon would be giving no information. Not in this life anyway. What he told to the angels . . . that would be between himself and his maker.

Longarm stood. So did Harney.

"Who shot him?" Longarm asked.

"Damned if I know. Me and Glenn was in the office talking things over. We heard the shot and came running. Found your prisoner on the floor. Whoever killed him must have shot through that window up there." He pointed toward a small window set high in the back wall of the jail.

Longarm tried to stand, then realized that Robby Brandon's dead hand still clutched at his sleeve. Very gently he disengaged the groping fingers and laid Brandon's hand down onto his chest. Then he was able to stand without hindrance. He turned and walked out.

The desk sergeant, Glenn something, was seated at his usual station in the office.

"Where's that doctor I asked you to fetch?" Longarm asked.

John looked up from a mail order catalog laid open on the desk. "Couldn't find him."

It had been only moments since Longarm asked for a doctor to be brought. Obviously John had not bothered to look for one.

Of course Brandon had been dying. That much had seemed obvious. But, dammit, sometimes men survived the most terrible of wounds. Or succumbed to the most minor of them. A doctor's assistance would have been appropriate, regardless of what any of them thought.

Not that there was any point in arguing about it now. Brandon was dead and gone. There was no coming back from that.

Longarm bit down on his cheroot and grabbed a lantern from a shelf in the police headquarters, not bothering to ask for permission. He gave it a quick shake to make sure it was filled with oil, lifted the bail, and struck a match.

He touched the flame to the wick and dropped the bail, then adjusted the wick to get a nice butterfly flame.

Glenn looked at him but said nothing when Longarm took the town's lantern outside.

He carried the lantern low, lighting his way around to the back of the jail. The window in the cell wall was easy enough to spot. Longarm ignored the window itself but did use the lantern to examine the ground beneath it. The soil was hard-packed, full of grit and soot and gravel.

Longarm stood under the window for only a moment. He could easily reach it. There was glass in a wooden frame on the outside of the cell bars. At the moment the window was pushed open, hinged at the top and propped open at the bottom. It could be manipulated, open or shut, from the inside.

Longarm heard footsteps approaching. He looked up to see Chief Harney.

"What are you looking for?" Harney demanded.

"Whatever there is to see," Longarm told him.

"Find anything?"

Longarm shook his head. The fat man paused to wipe his forehead, then set his hat back firmly onto his head and reached for the lantern. "That's mine, I believe." Longarm let him take the lantern. It was not worth arguing over.

Longarm started to walk away.

"Hey there, dammit," Harney snapped. "What about Brandon?"

Longarm stopped. Turned. "What about him?"

"Are you just going to leave him lying there?"

Longarm took the cheroot from his lips, turned it to examine the glowing tip for a moment, and tapped the ash off. He grunted, then said, "Yes. I am." He resumed walking toward the hotel.

Chapter 48

He was halfway back to the hotel when he remembered the reason he had gone to the jail to begin with. He still wanted to clean his .45, and they should have rags and some whale oil there. He turned around and went back the same way he had just come.

Longarm had to step aside to accommodate a pair of burly young men who were carrying Robby Brandon's sheet-draped body out to a waiting ambulance. Glenn had claimed he could not find a doctor when Longarm wanted one, but he obviously had no trouble getting an undertaker's assistants on short notice.

Longarm let the stretcher through, then went inside to find Chief Harney behind the desk. The fat police chief was busy cleaning his revolver just like Longarm intended to clean his. Longarm dragged a chair over by the desk and sat down uninvited.

"Mind if I use your cleanin' rod and oil an' such?"

"Don't mind at all," Harney said, giving his pistol a final swipe with an oily rag and slipping four shiny brass cartridges into the cylinder. He reached into his pocket to produce two more and dropped them in as well. "Help yourself," he said, snapping the revolver's loading gate closed.

The police chief returned the pistol to its holster and stood. "Here. Use this chair if you like."

"Why, thank you, Chief." Longarm was about half-surprised by the courtesy. But he accepted the offer and moved over to the comfortable swivel chair.

The cleaning materials were already laid out on the desk-top. Longarm unloaded his Colt and cleaned it, going over the firearm with meticulous care, then reloading. He pushed the .45 into its leather, tidied things on the desk, and looked around for the wastebasket so he could dispose of the dirty patches he had used in the barrel and in each of the six chambers.

The wastebasket was beside the desk. He hooked it to him with a toe and dropped the patches in.

In the bottom of the metal bin he noticed some papers. And two empty brass cartridge cases.

Longarm frowned. It was not that two pieces of brass were necessarily of any consequence.

But still . . .

Robby Brandon had been murdered with two well-placed shots to the chest.

And that cell window was awfully high up. Longarm himself was tall. He could reach the open window, but he was not tall enough to see through it without standing on something.

In that alley there had been no sign of anything a killer might have stood on to reach through and take aim at his victim.

Now these empty cartridge cases.

Longarm sat and stared toward the doorway where Chief Harney had disappeared only a few minutes earlier.

Harney? But *why*?

Longarm pulled out another cheroot and lighted it. It was his last cigar until he could buy some more. The mercantile was closed for the night, but perhaps they had some to sell over at the Tenpenny.

That was just one more reason for him to walk across the street to Ronald Harney's favorite saloon.

He shoved the wastebasket back where it belonged, called out to Glenn that he was leaving, and headed out into the night.

Tracks may lead someplace, Longarm reminded himself, but they make damned thin soup. What he needed now was meat. What he needed now was information.

Chapter 49

"Marshal. Could I see you for a minute?"

Longarm looked up to see the Evanston telegrapher Doug Baxter waving at him from the entrance to the café where Longarm was just about to sit down for breakfast. "Sure thing, Doug. Come join me. I'll enjoy the company."

"Oh, I can't stay. I need to get home and get some sleep. I've been on duty all night long, and I'm bushed."

"Coffee then?" Longarm offered.

"Thanks, but I'm really tired. I saw you come in here and wanted to catch up with you. Wanted you to know that I have your basket over at the depot."

Longarm frowned. "Basket? What basket?"

It was Baxter's turn to frown in consternation. "Why, the basket we've been hauling up and down the line for the past couple days. The one you said you wanted us to find and return."

Longarm laughed. "You mean Dewey Brannen's mama's basket. I'd forgot all about it."

"Maybe so, but I bet Dewey hasn't. Bet his mama won't let him."

Longarm shook his head. "Amazing. But thanks. I'll . . . You say it has been shuffling up and down the line?"

"Sure has. No one seemed to know quite what to do with it, so one crew would pass it off to another going the other way. You'd think we were playing some sort of shell game with Dewey's basket."

"All right then, Doug. I'll come by the depot and get it." He chuckled. "No idea what I'll do with . . . Oh, yes, I do. Don't worry. I'll take care of it."

Baxter went home to go to bed. Longarm sat at the counter and ordered a big breakfast. When he was done, he walked over to the Union Pacific depot. There, just as Doug had said, Dewey Brannen's mother's lunch basket was waiting for him.

It did not appear to have suffered much from its journey up and down the U.P. line. The red checked napkin was still wadded up inside it along with an apple core—a rather dark and mushy apple core by now—that Longarm had left there.

He took the basket, thanked the express agent on duty, and carried it over to a mercantile where he bought several yards of butcher paper and a ball of string.

His wrapping job was admittedly sloppy, but he got the job done, covering the basket and binding it with half the ball of string. Then he carried the resulting mess over to the post office, where he addressed it to Brannen, paid an exorbitant amount in postage, and saw the damn thing—napkin and all but without the apple core—off to Cheyenne.

By then he knew what he intended to do about the robbery of the United States mail and the murders of both Farley Oakes and Treasury Agent Beatrice Raven.

Chapter 50

"Mama, I want t'borrow one o' your girls. The prettiest one, eh? And, um, agreeable."

The little Chinese woman smiled and bowed. "Oh, yes, mister marshal man. So very happy to serve you, yes." She bowed again, grinning from ear to ear.

"An' I want t'buy a bolus of opium too. An' a pipe t'smoke it in," he said.

"Of course, mister marshal, but you know . . . you do what you want . . . but the opium takes away . . . how shall I say . . . makes less interest in pretty Chinese girl maybe so."

Longarm nodded. "Yeah, that's what I been told, but I'd like t'do it anyway."

"As you wish, mister marshal. As you wish."

"One more thing," he said. "I want to pay for the girl and the opium tar. This is official business and it's only right to pay."

"Official? Oh, my." The little woman covered her mouth with her hand and tittered behind it. "You wait. I get."

She disappeared into the smoky opium den and emerged a few minutes later with both the tools of her trade and, well, a tool of her other trade. She handed Longarm a pipe already

loaded with a walnut-sized ball of black opium tar, then
pointed to the breathtakingly lovely Chinese girl at her side.

"This is Kwei. She do whatever you want. Keep her long
time. She a good girl."

Kwei bowed low. The girl had pale, flawless skin. Huge
eyes. Black satin hair done up in a tight bun. Tiny breasts
and an impossibly small waist. She wore the standard red
silk dress with a gold pattern repeated on it. The dress was
slit up the side, exposing a pale, slender leg. She wore gold
slippers and had an ivory pick fastening her hair in place.
She was, Longarm had to admit, just about the prettiest thing
he had seen in many a moon.

It was just a damned shame he intended to use her in not
quite the way Mama Chen—and Kwei too—expected.

"Do you speak English?" he asked the girl.

She bowed and said, "I speak, yes."

"Then come with me. I got a job for you to do."

The girl giggled and followed, mincing along with tiny
steps, head down submissively, eyelashes dark against the
pallor of her skin. A good many Chinese, the laborers who
worked out in the sun in particular, Longarm had noticed,
had very dark skin. Not this girl. She was as pale as
porcelain.

And pretty. He could not help getting a hard-on just from
looking at her. The idea that he could do anything he wanted
with her . . . anything at all . . .

Not right now, unfortunately. He had work to do and she
was going to help him do it.

Longarm took the girl back to his hotel and brought her
upstairs to his room.

As soon as they entered the room, she slipped the dress
off over her head.

"No, no. Put it back on. You'll be going outside again in
a few minutes," he said.

The girl gave him a puzzled look, but she dropped the
dress over her shoulders and let it flow down her tiny body.

Longarm thought it a hell of a shame to cover anything so pretty, but it had to be done. For the moment.

"Do you know a man name of Glenn? Works as desk sergeant for the police chief. I don't know his last name."

"He is Mr. Harris. I know him."

"Has he, um, has he . . .?"

She laughed. "Has Mr. Glenn fuck me? No, never. He is with other girl. Never me. He cannot afford to pay for me." Her smile was dazzling. "I am number one pretty girl. Very 'spensive."

"How much d'you go for, Kwei?" he asked, genuinely curious now.

"I ten-dollar girl. Mr. Glenn always take one-dollar girl."

"But he has seen you?"

"Oh, yes. He take me with his eyes many time, never with his . . ." She mimed an erection at the front of her own flat belly.

"Perfect," Longarm said. "Now sit down here an' listen. Here's what I want you to do."

Chapter 51

Glenn Harris could hardly believe his great good fortune. How many times had he wanted this girl? Lusted for her? But could not afford to go with her. Now here she was, actually wanting *him*!

"So many time I wish you choose me, Mr. Glenn, so many. You always pick other girl. Now I pick. Take day off, yes? Pick you, please?"

She had taken him by the hand and led him to this room. Why, he did not even have to pay for the room. She had already done that, already had it waiting for the two of them. Incredible. Wonderful. Perfect.

Her name was Kwei. He already knew that. Had known it for a long time. A perfect China doll. Harris laughed with his own good fortune.

"No, not yet. First we smoke," she said.

"Hell, I don't want to smoke," Harris told her.

"Oh, yes, please. The pipe make me," she giggled, "better love girl. Put you in mood. Put me in mood. You smoke, please."

So what the hell. This was Kwei's fun as much as it would be his.

"Take off clothes. Lie here, please."

Kwei was already naked. She had slipped that dress off slick as skinning a cat. Lord, she was beautiful. Harris thought his dick might bust it was so hard.

"Take off, please. I help." And damned if she didn't too. Helped him with the buttons and the buckles. Knelt in front of him to pull his boots off. Smiled. Oh, she did smile. Beautiful.

"Lie here, yes."

She held the pipe to his lips. Struck the match for him. The first puff was harsh. He held it deep in his lungs and almost immediately felt the sweet, soothing effects of the opium softening the edges of the world and making him mellow.

"Oh, yes, Mr. Glenn. Here. Close you eyes." She laid a cool, damp washcloth over his eyes. Marvelous.

"Smoke. Yes." The girl's voice was as gentle as her touch. Glenn Harris felt so light he might float clean off the bed and bump into the ceiling.

"Oh, yes, very nice," the girl's sweet voice intoned. "Smoke is good, yes?"

Oh, the smoke was very good. Harris had not been this happy in . . . he could not remember how long. Ever. This was the best he'd ever in his life felt.

Kwei gently rubbed his temples. Wonderful!

He felt her weight shift and she seemed to be gone for a moment. Then she was back. She settled onto the very top of the bed. He inhaled her scent. She began rubbing his temples again, very lightly, and urging him to enjoy the pipe she presented to him. As if her own presence were not enough.

Glenn Harris was a very happy man.

Kwei briefly left Harris's side. She glided soundlessly to the hotel room door and opened it, letting Longarm in.

He followed her, tiptoeing back to the bed where she perched beside the naked, darkly hairy Glenn Harris and resumed rubbing his temples . . . and every once in a while very lightly brushing his cock with her fingertips as well. She kept the cool washcloth across his eyes, and every now and then Longarm would lean forward to whisper a question into her ear, a question that she would repeat aloud to Harris.

And he, eager to please and so horny his dick was throbbing, would answer her questions the very best he could.

"I know Chief Harney, he murder that Brandon man. I know that. It okey-dokey. Chief, he boss man. What he do is okey-dokey, yes. You saw. You there. I know you saw. You tell me, please. Tell me all. Here, sweet John. Take 'nother smoke. Now you tell me, yes?"

And Police Sergeant Glenn Harris did tell her, yes.

Chapter 52

Longarm walked into the Tenpenny, spotted Ronald Harney
at his usual table with his usual cronies, and approached the
fat man. "Excuse me, Chief. I need to have a word with you."

"Is this important, Long?"

"Yes, sir, it is."

"Well, spit it out then. What do you want this time?"

"Sir, this really has to be said in, well, in private." Longarm bobbed his head and spread his hands open in suppli-
cation. "I wouldn't ask you to come except that it's so
important."

The police chief pushed his chair back and laboriously
lifted himself out of it. A few more pounds of suet on that
frame, Longarm thought, and the man wouldn't be able to
waddle at all.

"Where are we going?" Harney asked.

"Just across to your office, sir," Longarm said.

"Shit, anything you can say to me you could as easy say
to one of my people."

"Not this," Longarm assured him.

"All right, then. All right. I'm coming."

The two made their way across from the Tenpenny saloon to Harney's police headquarters.

"Where is my sergeant? What in hell have you done with my sergeant?" Harney demanded when they got inside.

Longarm smiled. "He's in back. I took the liberty o' putting him there."

"Oh, all right. Let me . . . ah, shit . . . let me just sit here. You can pull that other chair over and tell me what is so important that you had to take me away from my card game." Harney wheezed as he lowered himself onto the sturdy desk chair.

"First," Longarm said, "let me . . ." He reached forward and snaked Harney's revolver away from the man.

"Hey now!"

"What this is," Longarm said, "is I'm sendin' you to the gallows. Or to a cell, your choice."

"I . . ."

"Shut up," Longarm snarled. "First you listen. Then you decide do you want to feel that rope around your neck or would you rather set in a jail cell for a good long time. It's a real choice. You might or might not know that murder ain't a federal crime. If I decide to charge you under our federal statutes, you'll go to Leavenworth and share a cell with some hairy son of a bitch that likes to ass fuck.

"Or I can have you charged under territorial law and you're pretty certain to hang for all the murders you done or were the cause of, startin' with Farley Oakes, includin' Bea Raven, who was a Treasury Department agent, an' leadin' to you bein' the cause of John Whitmore bein' killed, as well as probably some others that I can dig up if need be. Point is, you'll hang." Longarm snorted. "An' judging by your weight, the hangman will only need t'give you a real short drop when that gallows falls out from under your feet."

Harney cleared his throat and reached up to absently rub the side of his neck.

"That's about where the hangman's knot will hit you," Longarm said cheerfully. "If he does his job right, your fat neck will snap clean as breaking a stick o' peppermint candy in two." He grinned. "But you're the law your own self. You know all that, don't you?"

Harney snatched his hand away from the spot. "I don't know what you are talking about," he snapped.

"Of course you do. You and your police. The whole damn department. Intimidating poor Oakes until he agreed to help you. Taking advantage of Treasury giving you warning when shipments of cash come through. Then you heard . . . or somebody heard . . . about the printing plates being shipped, and that was just too much temptation to let pass by. Shit, you could just print up all the cash money you liked. Wouldn't have t'steal it or nothing.

"You browbeat poor Oakes . . . I guess he wasn't all that strong a man to begin with . . . you got him to let Glenn Harris go to Cheyenne and ride the train back from there. Got Oakes to open the door and hand over the mailbags containing the plates. Then Harris murdered the poor son of a bitch and you got away clean. Or thought you did.

"Now, the thing I don't know is where those plates are. What you done with 'em. Frankly, Chief, I don't all that much give a shit. I mean, we work for the same government an' all, but those printing plates are the responsibility of Treasury. What I came to do was to solve the mail robbery." Longarm smiled and chuckled. "An' I done that. By the way, if you're lookin' for your policemen, they're in back, locked up in one o' your cells. Which is where you'll join them when we're done talking. So you think over which you want, a hanging or Leavenworth. Then you an' me will talk some more. In the meantime I need to go over to the depot and send a couple wires. One to my boss down in Denver tellin' him what you an' me have just discussed. The other to the Treasury Department tellin' them who they need to see about getting their printing plates back. I expect some o' their people will be along directly to talk t'you about that."

Harney had turned pale as a leghorn chicken. His jowls

were trembling, and he looked like he might burst into tears at any moment. "Will it help if I give you the plates?"

Longarm slowly nodded. "It might. Might help some. For sure I'd tell it to the judge as hears your case. Can I take it you'd rather Leavenworth than a visit from the hangman?"

"Yes, I . . . Yes. You can assume that."

"Fine. Then reach right into that desk there for paper an' ink and write out a statement. Don't leave nobody out. Start from the beginning an' tell it all." Longarm smiled. "And in case you're wonderin', I already took your hideout gun outa the desk drawer. But if you're feelin' real brave, why, you go ahead an' do whatever seems right to you." His smile became positively evil.

Longarm waited for a good half hour or more while Ronald Harney wrote out his confession. Then he locked the chief in one of his own cells along with his own police officers and went over to the U.P. depot to take care of those telegrams. He was in something of a hurry by then, though.

Kwei was waiting for him at the hotel.

Watch for

LONGARM AND THE MOUNTAIN MANHUNT

the 406th novel in the exciting LONGARM
series from Jove

Coming in September!

GIANT-SIZED ADVENTURE FROM AVENGING ANGEL LONGARM.

BY TABOR EVANS

penguin.com/actionwesterns